Slice of Life

By Gene Hull

GOING TO COURT
  A Tennis Tribute

HOOKED ON A HORN
  Memoirs of a Recovered Musician

GENE HULL

Slice of Life

Our Ways and Days

*

Fiction Publishing, Inc.
Fort Pierce, Florida

Fiction Publishing, Inc
5626 Travelers Way
Ft. Pierce, Florida 34982

The characters and events in this book are fictitious.
Any similarity to real persons, living or dead, is
coincidental and not intended by the author.

An application to register this book for cataloging has
been submitted to the Library of Congress.

ISBN 13: 978-0-9814956-5-1
Printed in the United States of America

For

Sara, Amy, Rebecca, Margaret,
Christopher, Matthew, Peter and David,
who give me so much
to admire and live up to.

CONTENTS

Thank You   xi

Preface   xiii

San Francisco Triage...   1
        The Musician and the Lady

The Runner...   25
        And the Photographer

The Hike...   45
        New Hampshire Cure

Trapped...   65
        Buried Below

Caught...   95
        In Florida

The Flag...   107
        A Vermont Story

Tattoo...   117
        Forever or Not

Bird of Paradise...   147
    Miami Slice

The Beach....   159
    Life After Pennsylvania

Return of The Brave...   171
    Texas Homecoming

Kiss The Blarney Stone...   185
    The Quest

A Letter...   201
    In the Amazon Rainforest

About The Author   215

"Once we start looking for eyes, we find them everywhere, glinting at us, winking from every page."

Francine Prose

Thank You

Stories often have a way of attempting to go to sleep before their work is done. Some take their time finding their beds, dallying for yet one more re-write before being tucked in. So it has been with this collection.

Characters change. Plots twist. Dialogue freshens. Each time we write, we see them, listen to them. Revision follows revision.

With this in mind I want to thank fellow writers and family members who have graciously taken the time to read various drafts along the way and who in the process have offered suggestions that aided in revealing these characters and in finding comfortable homes for them.

I am sincerely grateful to all of you, especially Lynne Barrett for her insightful critiques of an important chapter and Amy Hull for her most conscientious editing.

And thank you, dear reader, for including in your interests the unique possibilities and enjoyments of short story forms.

Preface

Life-changing events happen, tiny and huge, light and dark, in the lives of everyone. Sometimes these are noticed by others, often only by those who live them. Slice of Life endeavors to recapture such moments through the subjective lens of prose.

If any unifying thread needs to connect these stories, let it be the commonality of self-absorption, the underlying catalyst that drives each of us toward our own destiny.

San Francisco Triage...
The Musician and the Lady_____

Leonardo sits at the bar in Opus Two. He looks comfortable enough sipping a tall draft waiting for the musicians to take the stage. He looks forward to sitting in and feels good about that. But by the time he finishes his third beer, he's brooding over Miami again. He's come clear across the country to get over it, but he knows he's not going to forget anytime soon. The pain is still there, and the hurt he carries doesn't get any lighter knowing she couldn't help it. He orders another beer.

He decides he's done with being nice for a while. Makes sense. Why bother? He lets self-pity stroke him. It feels good. He's got a right to be angry. Why not? He takes a long pull on his beer, enjoying the moment. Savors the taste of self-righteousness. At least now he's in a new place, a whole new world for him. It's 1986 and he's made it to San Francisco.

There is a sense of ritual he loves about good jazz clubs. There aren't many left these days, so when he finds one like this he appreciates the environment. To him these clubs are important mini-arenas for performing pure music, isolated from the din of pop music pap. Here he can be challenged to push his creativity to a higher level when he plays his horn, especially when audiences are true appreciators. And if performers and audiences give to each other, they both receive. It's a win-win situation. He likes the deal.

"So what's your story?" a woman seated beside him says.

Chatter from customers waiting for the music to begin backgrounds the room with a special charge, the kind of buzz that says the audience knows it's in for a treat.

Leonardo reflects on this, enjoys the anticipatory vibe. He's experienced it himself when seeing Miles and Mingus and Ellington and Woody's roaring big band. It's a special feeling.

He is dismissively aware of the woman. He knows she wasn't there when he first sat at the bar and chooses not to acknowledge her.

"What's your story?" she asks again.

Possibly she's assessing his blond hair or his almost boyish looks. After all, he's wearing his usual post-preppie garb, blue oxford button-down shirt, chinos and loafers. Not exactly hipster attire. But hey, you can be hip without being a hipster, right? He still doesn't look at her.

"Everybody's got one," she persists. "What's yours?"

He turns slowly and faces her, barricading himself behind a scowl. How come this person has chosen him to talk to when obviously he'd prefer to brood by himself? He glares a bit longer and responds with, "What?"

"Your story … you know."

"You *really* want to know?" he says with an edge. He knows his chip is showing.

"Look, my name's Irene," she says politely, extending her hand. "You seem to be troubled. Want to talk?" She appears to him to be in her late thirties or early forties—he really can't tell for sure—wears a smart beige business suit, coral scarf and heels. Not the usual sort you find in a bar; but then, this is a jazz club in a sophisticated city, not like the usual places where music is mostly just taken-for-granted stuff for socializing. Jazz appeals to people who want to listen and absorb.

He acknowledges her, offers her a perfunctory hand, then quickly disengages and says, "Look, I appreciate your asking, but who really gives a flying crap." It isn't a question. But it isn't like him to be crude either.

Almost immediately he says, "I apologize for that remark. I'm sorry. That was rude. Please, nothing personal." He quaffs his beer. Suds mustache him, accenting his hair and making him look a little older for a moment. "It's just that I don't see why anyone should be interested in me. Beside, I can't afford company."

She throws him a look. "You've got that wrong, buddy. I'm just trying to be friendly."

"Oh, sorry." So he made a mistake. So she's not a hooker. So? He still doesn't want to share personal thoughts with a stranger, especially an attractive older

3

woman. It wouldn't be right. Breaking up with his girlfriend is private business. Nothing he wants to talk about, especially in view of the way it happened. He knows he's acting grumpy, the mark of a needy man perhaps. He excuses himself and goes to the men's room.

When he returns, she waits until he is seated then says, "Who gives a *flying crap?* Well, maybe *I* do," matching his arrogance, and then some.

This gets his attention. Hmm, she's a feisty one. Not about to be bullied. Something is different.

"Oh, you do? And why would that be?"

"You look like a musician. I like musicians. I can relate to them."

He wants to believe her. But he has had it with women who say they can relate. He glances at the bandstand, then back at her. *She's just guessing.* "Well, *I-rene,* what makes you think I'm a musician?" He says this with a skeptical smirk. He can't believe he's being so crass. It's not his nature. But he really doesn't care what she says, doubting it will be true anyway. He's got her this time.

"Well, for one thing, smart ass, you walked in with a horn case."

His eyebrows arch. "Okay, I sure asked for that." His expression says he's been slam-dunked and is acting like a jerk. Come on stupid, try to be nice, he almost says aloud to himself. "Look, I just busted up with my girlfriend. To be honest with you, it decked me pretty hard. I'm just in a rotten mood."

"I'm sorry to hear that."

He hesitates to tell her how he really feels…how lack of acceptance is such a shrinking experience, especially for a musician. If people don't appreciate your music, you get down on yourself. But, okay, you can rationalize they just don't get it or don't know any better. Too bad for them. But inside you know you're just not communicating. You try all the harder to improve. Music is all about communication. But when you're rejected by the person you love, well, that's a whole different thing. It whacks the hell out of you, especially if it's not your fault. There's not much you can do about it. You have to press on, pump yourself up, tell yourself how good you are, even if you feel completely worthless.

He gulps more of his beer. The woman seems nice enough, and he really likes women. He shouldn't let a harmless chat with this Irene person 'fade to black,' even if he is in mourning. He should accept it for what it is and be happy an impressive woman wants to talk. Maybe he isn't a loser after all. And she does have a sense of humor. He'll keep it light.

"I'm really sorry for being so abrasive," he says politely. This time he gathers in what there is to see and likes it, especially her dark eyes.

"I think I understand how you feel," she says. "I could tell you're hurting."

He notices her figure. Hmm, nice, very nice. Okay, so maybe he'll flirt a little, just for practice. It can't hurt. He doesn't have to let this woman into his life. So what is he afraid of? He adopts a more positive approach and tries a modest trial balloon. "Do you think a nice lady like you should be talking to a complete stranger in a bar?" (Weak, he knows, but it'll have to do.) He says this with a mischievous twinkle, a habit he has when flirting, although he hasn't done it in a longtime.

She chuckles. "I'd trust a musician any day over most guys in a club."

"You would? In that case, I'm definitely a musician. Yeah, right. Damn right. Would you like a drink?"

"Chardonnay would be fine, thank you." Quietly he watches as the bartender pours.

So he was dumped. Well, not exactly. But he is an adult. He can handle it. Maybe it's time to let the past disappear, like a city left behind when you drive through a tunnel. Sometimes it's what you have to do when you start a new life. His face relaxes. He is relieved to focus on her, on someone new, even if he thinks he should be honoring his tragedy a little longer. If he really cares so much about his loss, why is he opening up to her? Shouldn't he continue brooding? Is this being disloyal? Aw shit, disloyal to whom? His ex-girlfriend doesn't care any more. Why should he?

There is a quality about this woman that makes him feel relaxed. Yeah, that's it, relaxed. And there's something else, something not to be taken lightly. The horns of desire have begun tooting their way into his psyche. Not exactly the song of a Siren, but he can hear them, faint as they may be. It's a guy thing.

"Bartender, a Chardonnay for the lady, please. Another beer for me."

"I dated a musician once," she says. "We lived together for a while. Good jazz player. I got to know how musicians think. He had this look about him, this I'm-vulnerable-but-sure-of-myself thing. I like that. I like men who are sure of themselves." She looks directly at him.

6

He doesn't feel too sure of himself at all. He lofts a fly ball for an easy catch. "Yeah, I guess some guys are like that."

She appears to think about this for a moment, then says, "I think most musicians are, once you get to know them."

"You think?" He is intrigued by her wise comments. And he likes the way she looks up and to one side, as if reaching for the precise expression of a thought. His mother used to do that.

"You can tell musicians," Irene says. "They have this, this look about them. Like you, for instance. You look like a former prep school guy, clean cut, neatly groomed hair, responsible looking, almost innocent, but you've got that look in your eye, that I'm-special look."

"I do? I don't think I've ever heard that before." He hasn't been feeling too special lately. "You writing a book?"

She laughs as if that could never be an option.

She *is* different, he concludes. Not some co-ed teasing you with a tight sweater and pouty lips, while trying to put you down with clever remarks—like that's supposed to make you try harder. She's older. Experienced. And very perceptive. He wants very much for her to like him, even if just for the moment. He'll settle for that. "Then how come you're not still with your musician guy?" he asks.

"Good question. It's just that I think musicians are special." She scans the room, tilts her head toward him and speaks in a confidential tone, "Well, he had this . . . this terrible temper and would get jealous the minute someone else talked to me. I'd tell him, 'don't be silly, we're just talking,' but he'd always make a scene."

7

"That wasn't too cool."

She looks around again, especially to where a few band members are seated with patrons. "There was definitely nothing cool about him coming off the bandstand one night in the middle of a set and smacking a nice guy who was only buying me a drink at the bar. Bloodied him for nothing."

"Wow."

"That convinced me. I told him it was over. Couldn't put up with his jealousy."

"Grim, man. I hate muscle stuff."

"Yes, I can tell that about you. You seem sensitive."

"I'd sure appreciate you if you were my lady. I'd stand by you. You're a classy person." Damn. Maybe he's blabbing too much. Besides, he isn't sure he means all that. Maybe it's the drinks. Nevertheless his instincts tell him she is a serious person with a sense of humor, and he can tell she likes men. That's good. After all, he's in a city where sexual preferences can't be taken for granted, and this really nice woman is attracted to him, right?

"Thank you. I have a certain feeling about you too," she says."

Oh, God, yes. "Have another drink?" With raised eyebrows he nods toward the bartender. Holds up two fingers.

"Okay, but I'm buying," she insists. She finishes the wine left in her glass and sets it down slowly. "Musicians appreciate women. They like to be romantic and think they're sexy. It's tender in a way. Of course, sooner or later some new looker comes by and tells them how wonderful they are, bats her eyes and wiggles her ass. The next thing, 'Honey, I need some space.' But in the meantime, when musicians are on, they're fun and romantic. And when they're down, something about them makes you want to help them feel better."

Whoa. Is she talking about sex? Maybe. He'd better be cool. He doesn't know if he's ready for that yet. But his interest is definitely piqued.

"I can kind of relate to what you're saying. Like I said, I'd sure appreciate you. The guy you were talking about was just an ignorant jerk. There are always idiots like that." He looks at her with a puppy expression. "You have a beautiful smile and you seem so together. Are all the women in San Francisco as open as you?"

"Thank you," she says. "That's sweet of you to notice. I can't speak for all women. It's just my way."

He knows the nice part of alcohol is permitting him to be more expressive. But after all, he is an enlightened person. So why not be honest? It's nice to be articulate in a high-level conversation like this. The more he talks, the quicker he gulps. He downs another beer.

Irene sits on the high stool with legs crossed, a knee resting against him, which manages to expose a generous helping of thigh. He wonders how it would be to touch her leg right now. No, of course he wouldn't do that. He's cool. Just thinking about it. Hmm. So what if she's coming on to him a little? He deserves it, especially after what happened in Miami.

"So come on now, tell me," she says, "it's your turn. What's your story?"

"You really want to know?" He gives her a cocky smile.

That phrase again. They both laugh at it. It relaxes them.

"I told you mine...." She gives his knee a playful squeeze.

"Okay. First off, I play tenor sax. To me it's the closest instrument to the human voice."

"I love the sax," she interjects. She doesn't remove her hand from his knee. He feels a shiver. It's been months.

"My name's Leonardo."

"I was waiting for you to tell me."

"Sorry. And by the way, it's never Leo. Always Leonardo."

"That's so cool," she says, nodding and re-sounding his name, holding the last syllable and pouting her lips. *Leonardo-o-o-o-o.*

He pauses, looks intently at her. "You sure have beautiful hips. LIPS! Whoops. Sorry." Damn.

She smiles, noticing him blush. "Why were you named Leonardo? Must be a story there. Your father?"

He looks at her lips again. Whew. "No. My mother is an artist and wanted me to be one too. I think she thought the name would be some kind of iconic influence on me."

"Well, in a sense it has been, right?"

Leonardo shrugs, accepting the compliment, or at least the observation. "I think playing jazz is right up there with the best of art. You have to create new music every time you play. "Out of the corner of his eye he is aware of two band members doing their see-you-after-the-set farewells, kneading their ladies' shoulders. They leave the table and make their way toward the bandstand, talking, laughing. One is a huge guy carrying a trumpet. Leonardo turns and looks toward them for a moment.

As they saunter he notices that mini-spotlights are making a vain effort to illuminate the slightly raised stage area. Why the hell don't they put the right amount of light on the musicians? Club owners try to save money in the dumbest ways. After all, the musicians are the attraction. Why not light them up so people can see them?

He doesn't notice Irene watching him intently.

"You see," he says, turning back to her, "there's an underlying harmonic structure to jazz improvisation. Not just playing around, you know? It's stimulating, intellectual. It's art. It takes real study and commitment. Why are you smiling?"

"You're lecturing the choir. I told you. I know musicians. Always serious, always on a mission to be somebody."

"I guess this all sounds familiar to you then, huh?"

She looks at him, raises a shoulder, arches her eyebrows, glides her head to one side, as if to say, Well?

"Yeah, right," he says. "Anyway, as long as I'm in San Francisco, I'm going to catch Dexter Gordon. I hear he's back from Europe. Pretty old now, but one of the greatest sax players ever. I've got most of his records. When he plays, I don't hear notes coming out of his horn. I hear *him*. Oh, sorry if I'm bending your ear. Haven't had a conversation with a real woman in a long time, especially about music, and never with one like you." He can't wait to sit in with the band to show her how well he plays. Guaranteed strokes.

"I love listening to you talk," she says. "You're so sincere. Now come on, tell me what happened."

She listens as he unwraps the Miami story, starting with the night the band he was working with folded....

11

Driving thirteen hours from Charlotte straight through to Miami, he stopped only to gas up and use restrooms. It was late by the time he reached her apartment in Coconut Grove. His twenty-two-year-old girlfriend wasn't expecting him for three more weeks. He knew she'd be overjoyed to see him and he decided to stage a 'surprise, honey' entrance.

He had a plan: tiptoe into her bedroom, place a rose on her pillow and kiss her forehead lightly. He'd stoke her hair softly then caress her lips with his. He'd be so gentle. She'd coo in the special way she did when she was half asleep, feeling cozy and loving. Her warm lips would open to his and she'd reach up and pull him down to her. And all would be well.

When he reached her apartment he let himself in and closed the door quietly behind him. Her bedroom door was slightly ajar. He paused, savoring the moment. He heard quiet music. Candlelight flickered shadows against a far wall. She didn't usually light candles. He swung the door open slowly.

She and another young woman were in bed making passionate love, eyes closed, unaware of anything else. For a moment he thought he was hallucinating, over-tired from the long drive. But he knew what was happening, just as surely as if someone punched him in the stomach. His face twisted. He considered dumping the bed over. His six-foot frame could have accomplished this easily. He felt he needed to do something, anything. Yell. Swear. Slam something. But what good would that do? Instead, too shaken and shocked to speak, he withdrew unnoticed, and left, going back to his apartment.

Leonardo doesn't tell Irene what happened next but he remembers it vividly ... how he drove to his apartment, opened the sax case, took out his tenor and walked into a dark closet. He shut his eyes and poured pain and disillusionment into the horn, burying the wide bell into hanging clothes to muffle the sound from neighbors. Passionate cadenzas surged out, furious statements that gave way to fat-bellied, soulful sounds. Then came howls from the highest registers of the horn, explosions that segued magically into lyrical melodies. Soon, as if unable to tolerate any trace of sensitivity, he launched into crude, almost belligerent honking right down to the very bottom of the tenor. Ugly, vulgar sounds. He played for hours with no rhyme or reason. Until he was exhausted. Until he had gotten it all out of his system. Until there was no more to say. A few weeks later he left for San Francisco.

Leonardo relives this part of the story in private. He loses himself in anguish until her upbeat voice says, "At least you both know the truth now. It was good that it happened." Her eyes brighten. "Bet you were surprised. Why didn't you jump in bed with them?" She says this not in jest, but as if it might have been a logical option.

"Look, it wasn't a game. We were in love and love is sacred. Besides, I'm not into that sort of thing. I was, like, dumbfounded. I thought we had a future."

"Well, some women like women, too."

"Yeah, I can understand that. No problem. But not her. I had no idea she was in love with her girlfriend."

Irene's eyes sparkle as she teases, "Did you feel like smacking her in the face and hitting her girlfriend over the head with your horn?"

"Yeah, sure. Naw, that never occurred to me. I was just too numb. I didn't yell or make a scene. I hate that stuff. And actually, you're right. It is better I found out the truth, even if it was a shocker. Like I said, I slipped out of her place quietly. But boy, it doesn't do much for your ego when you get dumped like that."

"Aw, poor baby," she says, as only a woman can who is comforting her man or a child with a boo-boo. "Believe me, it's not the end of the world." She snugs her barstool closer to his and moves her hand from his knee to his thigh, stroking him lightly as if calming a puppy, careful not to dig in with her manicured fingernails, the coral polish of which match her scarf. "What amazing restraint you showed, Leonardo. You're so gentle. Mind me asking how old you are?"

"Twenty-four. Anyway, there was no reason for me to stay in Miami, I hopped in my car. Thought I'd make a fresh start somewhere. Kept going till I got here to San Francisco, the farthest I could get from Florida. I'd like to stay here. But to tell the truth, it seems expensive. Have to find a gig soon." He looks at her, searching her eyes. She understands him. Sure, that's it.

"When did you get here?" she asks.

"A week ago."

"Where are you staying?"

"Just for fun, I thought I'd stay in the park tonight with the ex-Flower People, over by the Golden Gate Bridge. I hear it's safe. I'll save a few bucks. Besides, it's a beautiful night. I've got a cousin in Phoenix. Maybe I'll head there after a while. But this is a great town for music. By the way, what time does the band start playing in this club? I hear they're dynamite."

"Ten-thirty. Pretty soon. And they're good, all right."

"I'm going see if I can sit in."

"Should be no problem. Lots of guys sit in." She fiddles with her scarf then fingers the rhinestone pin on her jacket. "Leonardo, would you excuse me for a moment while I go to the ladies room?"

"Of course."

She gets up, enters the hallway where the telephones are.

When she returns the bartender smiles and places two glasses of white wine in front of them. She puts a twenty on the bar. Leonardo continues his story, nonchalantly reaching for his wine. "I was in a department store a few days ago, kind of an upscale place, across the street from the St. Francis Hotel. Man, did I get stares from women passing me in a different direction on the escalators." He sips. "They really size you up. Took me awhile to put it together. Guess they were trying to figure me out. Was I or wasn't I? I felt like nodding to them and saying Don't worry, I'm straight."

"I don't blame them. It's the Eighties. A girl has to be sure these days. Saves a lot of disappointment later. You know, Leonardo, I'm feeling a little jealous…you getting the once-over by strange women and all." She crinkles her nose at him, playfully touching his. "I feel like I know you much better than they do."

Leonardo gulps down the wine. "Hmm," he says, mulling over his announced intention to sit in and meet the musicians. He has to consider his undeniable arousal and the immediate possibilities with this woman. Meekly he offers, "Too bad I'm going to sit in with the band tonight." It's almost an apology.

15

"Oh, that's right," she says.

A petite redhead comes in, sweeps the bar scene with her eyes and heads toward them. She fills a black cocktail dress nicely, Leonardo notes, wears her makeup lightly and has a ready smile. Another proper lady, he observes, as she walks over to them.

"Hi, Irene," she says, "who's your handsome friend?"

"Sophie! What a nice surprise. This is Leonardo. Leonardo, this is my apartment mate. He's a musician, Sophie."

"Ooh, what a nice name, and what a handsome young man."

Hmm, she's attractive, too … probably about Irene's age. A looker. He sits up straighter on his bar stool.

"He plays sax," Irene says.

"Oh, I *love* the sax, Leonardo. It's so nice to meet you." Her eyes fix on his, which are wide open and getting a bit glassy. She smiles with deep meaning, or so it seems to him, and squeezes his hand.

"Sophie, why don't you join us?" Irene invites. "Just remember I saw him first."

"Oh, sure," Sophie responds, overdoing a chuckle.

The two women flank Leonardo and nudge their seats even closer to him. "Three white wines, please," Sophie says to the bartender, "Chardonnay." Then to the other two, she adds, "My treat."

Leonardo expands with contentment. "Bet nice women like you in this town are loyal to their guys, huh?" The women nod with a questioning look. "You know, maybe that's part of the reason I came out here, not just for the moozit, I mean the music." He blinks slowly a few times. "Women are like music to me. Every time I play my tenor I think about a woman." He isn't sure if he really believes that, but it sounds good. Actually there is some kind of connection there, though he's never quite figured it out.

Irene smiles. "Ooh, I like that."

"Oh yes, so do I," says Sophie.

The bartender sets three wines on the polyurethaned redwood bar. "Cheers," the women say, raising glasses, looking at Leonardo.

"Whoa, thanks. This is so cool." He lifts his glass to Irene, nods. Then to Sophie, the same. "Wow, what a town. Should have come here before."

He is aware the rest of the band has made their way onto the stage. He hears flights of guitar notes interspersed with trumpet doodling. The drummer paradiddles around his set. But none of that seems quite as important to Leonardo now. More primal instincts are subduing his artistic inclinations, disturbing the fit of his pants. He squirms, hunches over toward the bar to make an adjustment. His direction finder is seriously awake. So what? That doesn't mean he has to follow wherever it points. Or does it? No way. He's come here to sit in with the band and make contacts.

"Sophie, Leonardo was just telling me he doesn't like that macho stuff. He's a gentleman. Isn't that right, Leonardo?"

"Well, yeah. It's just that I can't see any sense in that macho stuff."

"That's so wise," says Sophie.

"Mind if I ask you something, Leonardo?" Irene says, almost in a whisper, leaning toward him.

"Sure, Irene."

"You seem like such an honest guy, and so sweet. Would you like to stay at my place tonight?"

"Stay at your place," he blurts aloud, "with *you*?" (The bartender muffles a guffaw.) "That's very considerate, but you hardly know me. You sure?"

"I can tell about people and you're really nice." She wraps an arm around his neck, flicks her tongue lightly in his ear then gives him a long kiss.

Whew. That does it. He responds in kind with sincere Budweiser passion, upgraded by the Mondavi Chardonnay. So much for his broken heart. He doesn't understand why he feels so much better. He should feel guilty. Ah, screw it. He accepts the scene as some kind of divine intervention. "Well, since you put it that way, I'd love to stay at your place, right after I sit in with the band. You sure your roommate here won't mind?"

"Me?" Sophie interjects. "Oh, don't worry about me. I have my own room. You two have fun."

Irene whispers into his ear, "Leonardo, you know I've got such a special feeling about you."

"Wow," he says like a kid, "San Francisco's a great place; and I haven't even heard Dexter Gordon yet. Nice wine, too. Umm, I'm going to have another. Want one?"

"Sure." Sophie says. "I'm buying." Irene declines.

On the bandstand the musicians open the set with an extended version of "Green Dolphin Street", a jazz evergreen. Reassuring ripples of applause greet the group as the audience recognizes the main theme and settles in to enjoy the moment as if savoring a dinner about to be served. Each player solos in turn. The sounds are sensitive and lyrical. The big trumpet player, however, builds his lengthy solo with forceful passion.

"Outta sight," Leonardo says.

Irene, observing his fixation, gives his thigh a special squeeze.

The musical arrangement climaxes in a repeated rhythmic pattern as the bass player drones on a low E. Over this pulsing hypnotic bed Mr. Huge Trumpet Man improvises freely with a beautiful stream of notes, climbing higher and higher until at length he soars high above the band. He gets to the crowd. They applaud in rapture. The group's rendition of the piece lasts over fifteen minutes.

"Wow," Leonardo says, shaking his head in amazement. He turns and smiles at Irene.

The musicians acknowledge the applause then embark on the Dizzy Gillespie-Charlie Parker classic, "A Night In Tunisia". The intensity stirs the very roots of the room. The crowd moves, sways. Some keep time with their feet, others pat their knees or snap their fingers in sync with the beat. A few stare transfixed. In one way or another everyone grooves into the mesmerizing pulse, becoming one with the music. Another huge hand at the end of the number. Leonard can't stop applauding. Irene observes him carefully.

The piano player begins playing a pensive solo ballad, an interlude between numbers. The crowd hushes. The other musicians stand to the side and listen to him.

"Boy, are they hot," Leonardo says to her.

"I told you they were good."

He gestures expansively, unevenly, as if a little fuzzy, "So. How did your musician boyfriend take to you brushing him off when you told him good bye?"

"To tell you the truth, now that I'm not interested in him anymore, he's after me again."

"Figures. Guys always want what they can't have. They're stupid. They just don't understand women." My, how he has matured in the past hour.

"You're so wise, Leonardo. The jealousy thing is flattering at first, but it can get dangerous. He would get out of control so easily, like a madman; it was frightening."

"Oh yes," Sophie chimes in. "He was like a madman. He played guitar."

"Trumpet!" says Irene, raising her eyes at Sophie and nodding toward the big trumpet player.

"Right. *Trumpet*! A mean guy, all right. What a temper." She looks at Irene and waits for her lead. Leonardo misses the interaction.

Irene raises her wine glass, her little finger declaring independence from her delicate hold on the stem. She points casually across the room and says, "As a matter of fact, Leonardo, that's *him* on the stage." She nods toward the band, raises her eyebrows a bit, as if to say How about that? She holds her glass to her mouth for some time. Over the rim, her eyes watch Leonardo trace the path she has indicated toward the bandstand.

"Over there?" says Leonardo. "The big guy? The dynamite big trumpet player? In the band?"

"That's right," Irene offers.

"Oh, he's really a mean bastard," Sophie chimes again. She presses Irene's arm.

Leonardo stares toward the trumpet player, who could be a linebacker for the Raiders. His warning system begins to beep. It picks up intensity, gradually penetrating the blissful security of the alcohol. Leonardo's pulse accelerates to condition red. He recognizes the feeling and knows what he has to do. He is in no mood to have his teeth rearranged or his head bashed. He says with a false yawn, "Irene, whaddaya say we cut out now and go to your place. I, I can sit in tomorrow night. I'm kind of tired anyway." He gulps down the rest of his wine.

"Fine with me, Leonardo. Whatever you say."

He turns to Sophie. "Nice to meet you, Sophrie."

"The pleasure's all mine, Leonardo. You're sweet."

Leonardo and Irene get up. His sax case bumps into a few bar customers as he weaves his way to the door, Irene in tow. "Oh, sorry. 'Scuse us," she offers.

"'Night, kids, have fun," Sophie calls after them. "I'm going to hang out here." The band starts another set.

Outside, sounds of jazz fade as a cable car clangs past the club on its way down the long hill. Far below, bay mist rolls into Ghiradelli Square, at first sparing rooftops and chimneys, then swirling up and enveloping all in its fist. Except for the distant crooning of foghorns, the city grows quiet. But not everyone is thinking of sleep.

The stereo system wallpapers Irene's candlelit bedroom with the elegant tenor sax sounds of Stan Getz sonorously wooing "The Girl From Ipanema". Before very long, Leonardo is losing himself in the folds of wonderland. What bliss could be better than this.

Sometime within the next hour he emerges from his euphoric state, surprised that he feels a little guilty. Something isn't right. Although he enjoys immensely what is happening and is truly grateful, he doesn't relish the dependence it implies. He feels like a welfare patient … and he's only twenty-four. He's too young to be a charity case.

21

Even if she is a practitioner of nature's wondrous healing art, it's likely she's just taking pity on a young guy who's moaning about his lost love. Yeah, she feels sorry for him, that's it. So some degree of maternal compassion factors in—he is aware of the age difference. Okay, he can live with it. But he doesn't want it to be like that.

He knows what the problem is. He is being a taker. Not his style. It's got to be a win-win situation. Like when he's playing for an audience. *Quid pro quo*, right?

He rolls away slightly as if to light a cigarette, but doesn't. His mind tumbles with possibilities until the reality of it all becomes clear. Both he and this lovely stranger-woman are assuaging their own emptiness, as well as each other's. Neither one is taker or giver. Each is both. He is not the only one who's been wounded. It's like she's telling him Remember yesterday, but it's all right to live today. Sometimes sharing each other is the only way to make it through.

He turns to her with an expression of relief.

His desire renews as yet another realization occurs to him. This is more than a casual mutual-healing. True feelings are involved here. He can tell. He smiles as they embrace one another again, locking together. She is truly wonderful. The electricity of *love* shivers him. She murmurs, "Oh, yes." He knows she cares deeply for him … just as he does for her. Maybe she even loves him. It's a glorious moment of truth, a one-to-one symbiotic connection, one of life's improbable miracles. He can't believe he is so lucky to have found her.

"I, I think I love you," he murmurs.

"Oh, Leonardo…."

It is the stuff of songs.
Maybe he'll write one about it later.

Leonardo doesn't notice as Sophie, naked, tiptoes into the bedroom.

**

The Runner...
And the Photographer_____

Warren sits on the long wooden steps of the
boathouse with a group of colorful seniors who are
much farther along than his forty-two years. He enjoys
their company. It's his favorite perch when he comes to
the park, usually on Sundays, always alone. Since his
divorce a few years ago, the park is a place for him to
reassure himself that life is a beautiful thing, if one
focuses on the beauty not the woe. He considers the
scene there a veritable *Sunday In The Park* as Seurat
might have painted it today—joggers puffing along
October leafy trails, boaters, picnickers, a panoply of
people-at-play—a bucolic respite from city life. It's a
quick fix for him.

    "Track," he hears a woman call out on a distant
path. He watches as she approaches slower runners.
Joggers do not just slow down and move to the side,
letting the faster runner pass, as is the usual courtesy.

Instead, they pull off the path, stop, clear the way and watch as she breezes by at an incredibly smooth pace. Exercisers and game-players alike interrupt their routines to gawk with appreciation.

Now that's different, he reflects, especially in *this* park, in *this* city, which has seen everything. She is no ordinary Sunday-in-the-park runner. This elegant, lithesome woman in the yellow tank top and blue shorts cruises swiftly in and out of view along the lakeside path displaying exquisite form, a gorgeously fluid, natural style.

Warren knows about running. Years ago he was a cross-country runner at Indiana State University. For him there was no freer feeling in the world than loping briskly across the quiet, open countryside. Now, still trim, but left with two cartilage-worn knees, he knows he's lucky to be walking, and resigns himself to observing others and workouts in the gym. No wonder he admires, even envies, the young woman as he watches her, fascinated by such poetic motion, a body in perfect balance.

He really should capture the moment. He picks up his high-speed digital camera and hurries to the other side of the lake. On the way, in-line skaters sway past him on the sidewalk. Lovers on blankets raise wineglasses. A Frisbee gets snatched from the air by an acrobatic dog that almost runs into him. The dog drops the Frisbee, pants at him. Warren picks it up and scales it out on a lofty arc. "Go get 'em, tiger." Yeah, he loves this place. He hurries on.

He notices a group of young men and women playing touch football in a field. They exude the *joie de vivre* of a Budweiser commercial. He takes a few quick pictures of them. It must be nice to have so many fun friends. He wonders if television commercials imitate real life or do people emulate the commercials?

He crosses the stone-arched walking-bridge and finds a spot where the jogging path narrows, as it rounds a high cropping of gray boulders before resolving into a long straight-a-way. He takes a position near the top and waits to get a better look at her.

Here she comes. He readies his Nikon D2, concentrates on her every move, and begins clicking.

She has the form of an Olympian at least (click), an extraordinarily beautiful one at that (click), an athletic ideal (click). Look at that long stride (click), the relaxed breathing. And what a fine glowing face (click). His photographer's-eye doesn't miss a detail.

He notices how her shapely body instinctively leans (click) as she slows to carve the curve around the rocky overhang where he sits. He has an urge to call out, "Hey, Hello, Hi," or "You look great," or something, anything. But he doesn't. It would violate the moment. Excelsior, he says to himself as she effortlessly accelerates onto the straight-a-way (click, click, click).

The young woman's long, tawny hair, flowing freely behind her, is a picture in itself. He imagines her in a double exposure, superimposed over a sailboat skimming along a foamy blue sea with a golden pennant atop its mast. The park is the perfect gallery for her. Who is she?

He makes his way back to the boathouse where sun worshippers are getting their weekly dose of Vitamin D. His small group of senior cronies, two of whom are enjoying cigars, are still relaxing on the steps watching everybody. Each week they gather and exchange definitive opinions, acting like adjudicators of the best and worst of show. They always manage to argue about their selections. Warren enjoys them and listening to their banter, but he usually doesn't enter into their discussions.

"Hey guys," directing his question to no one person in particular, but to the general center of the group, "I was wondering if any of you know who that blonde young woman in the yellow and blue is? I don't remember seeing her before?"

"Well, you haven't been around in a while," says Milton. He's a charcoal-bearded seventy-year-old wearing gray sweats, an extra large Yankees shirt, tennis shoes and a blue beret. Milton always seems to know what's going on. He long-draws on a Corona, puffs out ringed billows with the aplomb of George Burns, and says, "Yeah, she's a beauty, all right. Started running here a few months ago."

He's one of those types whose business it is to know everyone else's business. "And she isn't on the Olympic Team, either, if that's what you're thinking, though she sure looks like it. I've seen them all and she's right up there with the best of them. Know what else? This'll kill ya. She's the new principal flutist with the Philharmonic. Came here from the Dallas Symphony. How 'bout that?"

"Yeah," an eager member of the unofficial voyeurs club adds, implying Milton isn't the only one who knows stuff. "Her name is Leslie ... something."

"Leslie Read," Milton says, re-asserting his position as the main man in the know." She's thirty and not married."

"Miltie, you amaze me," says Warren. How do ou find out all this stuff?"

"It's what I do." he drains another drag on his stogie.

Before Warren can say anything else, other guys add their comments, as if they share in Milton's social omniscience."

"She sure is a sweetie," Louie says. "One day she cruised by, gave us a big smile and a real nice Hello."

"I could watch her all day," Red adds. His hair is white. Warren figures Red is a nickname from a more colorful past. "She's got it all. Smart, too. I can tell. She'd be just right for my son."

"You mean your grandson," pops Milton.

"Alright already," Red says.

Warren nods. "Hmm, pretty incredible, guys, an accomplished musician, runs great, goddess looks, mesmerizes everybody, and I've never seen her before."

"Well you haven't been around much, like I said," says Milton. "What do you expect? You taking pictures today, Warren?"

"A few. I'd sure like to get more of her, though."

"I bet you would," says Red.

"Me too," grunts Henry, "a lot more."

Warren hangs out with them a while longer but doesn't see any trace of the runner. He gathers his gear and strolls across the park taking a short cut through the woods to an exit.

He stops a few yards off one of the more secluded running paths to have a much-unneeded cigarette. He's just about to light up, leaning against a shady elm, when he spots a big guy with the bulk of an ex-NFL tackle wanna-be chugging along, unevenly, almost weaving along the trail. The man exudes the kind of bravura that is at once unnerving to others; strangers would sense the advisability of giving him a wide berth.

From his secluded spot Warren has a clear view. He lifts his camera to get a shot of Big Foot (click, click). The bruiser appears to have had at least one too many (click), sings (in a manner of speaking) loudly off key. Ow. No respect for nature *or* music. Oh well, it takes all kinds.

From the other direction, beyond the path's blind curve, Warren hears, "Track!" It's her. She rounds the bend and sees the big galoot facing her ahead. Again she calls out, "Track."

The man looks up and stops. Instead of getting out of the way he spreads out his gorilla arms, straddles the trail, blocks her way. He smirks, sways unsteadily and says, "Hey, Bay-bee … come to Poppa!"

Warren clicks again then decides this could be trouble for the girl. He'd better get over there. But she closes the distance too fast for Warren to move. She's in full view now.

She eyes the big slob with a wry smile, as if inviting him, then heads directly for him at half speed. (click).

The galoot undulates his hips in anticipation. "Yeah, baby!" (click). A few yards from him, however, she makes a quick head fake to the right, then one to the left, then cuts sharply to the right, darting around him, never breaking stride, completely faking him out (click, click).

"Bye, bye, *Poppa!*" she calls, as she whizzes by. He clutches vainly at the air.

"*Bitch,*" he yells, whirling about, tangle-footed, looking after her. She fades into the distance so fast he could have thought she was a yellow and blue Harley.

Warren laughs quietly. "You go girl," he mutters, "beauty and balls."

As Warren exits the park he sees her talking to a cop on the sidewalk. He approaches them.

"Well, ma'am," the cop is saying, "there's all kinds of jerks in the park. Sometimes you take your chances in there. Look, the guy was probably just kidding around. But I'll make a report."

"Oh really? And that's all you're going to do? It's supposed to be safe in the ..."

"Officer," interrupts Warren, "you don't understand. This guy was going to grab her. Blocked her way. I'm sure he would have grabbed her."

"Oh yeah? You see it happen?" says the cop to Warren. "You know this for sure?"

"Look at these pictures. They ought to convince you." Warren cues up his Nikon and displays the pictures of the encounter the galoot.

"Ah-ha. Yeah, we know this guy. Didn't think he was around anymore. We'll pick him up and see that he gets banned from the park."

"And that's it?" says Leslie.

"Lady, it's all I can do. We'll take care of it. No real crime was committed." He hands the camera back to Warren, takes their names and addresses, notes the time, and walks away.

Leslie looks at Warren and says with concern, "Sir, may I see those pictures please?" He hands the camera to her. She frowns then smiles at her close encounter with possible disaster. "How did you happen to take these?"

"I was in the park, ah, walking through. I saw him just before you came running around the curve. By the way, that was some trick you pulled, the way you avoided him. Pretty risky, though. But if you didn't make it, I was ready to jump on him. You saved me from having to wrestle a polar bear. Thanks." He chuckles unconvincingly. Extending his hand he says, "Hi, my name is Warren Duphiney."

"Thank you, Warren. Nice to meet you. I'm Leslie. That's an interesting way to look at it … me saving you. I could imagine tangling with that guy would have been no fun. That's why I went for it."

"You live around here?"

"Not far. Over on the West Side."

"Well, usually when a knight charges forth to rescue the princess from an ogre, they live happily ever after. But of course you galloped away before the prince had a chance to save you. Some gallop too. Have no fear, though, I was ready." He laughs at his own remarks and begins to blush.

She smiles, not missing anything, right into his eyes. "Thanks. I do thank you, really. Your timing was terrific. The cop didn't believe me."

"Well, you know how photographers are. Always seem to be around when you don't want them. But this was luck today. I'm really a portrait photographer and do a lot of commercial work. I'd love to do some studio portraits of you. I'm sure you'd love them. No charge. Really." He hands her his business card.

She looks at it. "Oh, I don't know about that. But I do thank you very much for speaking up to the officer. And I do appreciate your comments about my running."

"You're some runner, Leslie. I used to run in college. You've got talent."

"Why thank you, Warren. Careful, you'll make me blush. I did too. But it's just a hobby now, whenever I have some free time. Speaking of which, I really have to go. I have a rehearsal. She shakes his hand. "Thanks again," she says not avoiding his eyes. "Bye now."

She starts to jog away.

"Hey, what's your last name," he calls.

She turns and says, "Leslie Read."

"Bye, Leslie Read." He watches till she vanishes around a corner two blocks away. Warren can't believe it. He hasn't talked so easily to a woman since his divorce three years ago. He can't he was so glib. What a lovely person.

He finds her number in the phone book as soon as he gets home. She's on West 83rd.

Two weeks go by. He doesn't call her, though he really wants too. Most likely he'd sound like he's coming on to her and she'd fluff him off. And that would kill him. He can't bring himself to start up with another woman, even just a phone call. It would only end badly again. Just can't do it. Then an idea strikes him. He thinks it over. It could work.

The next morning, full of resolve, he calls his old friend Larry Bishop. *PR Larry* has lately been handling Marketing and Promotion for the Philharmonic. He's a bundle of energy. Ideas fly off him like pigeons scattered by five-year-olds. "There isn't anything that can't be promoted," Larry likes to say.

"Larry, I've got an idea for you," Warren bubbles.

"Yeah?"

"You always say Symphony Orchestras need promoting, right?"

"That's true. Most orchestras are in trouble these days. People aren't supporting them like they used to, even though they say they want the music."

"Well, they advertise, don't they?"

"Sure, but their marketing strategies got mostly of touch. For a while there, ads read like formal library posters. No pizzazz. Kept talking to the same people, the ones who went to concerts anyway. You can't grow an audience like that. Things have changed. Here's the way it is. People spend money on whatever they think they can't live without, even if it's a frill. So you've got to make the public feel that if they don't buy it, whatever it is you're selling, they're missing out on the real action. And that's the one thing they can't stand in this town ... being left out."

"I know, I know. And that's just why I'm calling."

"Oh, really? So what's your idea?"

Warren calms himself. "I want to do a photo shoot of the Philharmonic's new principal flute player."

"This is your big idea? What the hell for?"

"Some promotions work because the public loves to look at beautiful women, especially if they're interesting and smart. "

"Uh-huh. So? Tell me something I don't know. Where you going with this?"

"Larry, you should have a *Miss Philharmonic*."

"A what? You nuts? Get real. This isn't beer or subways or television. We're talking one of the world's great cultural institutions, the National Philharmonic, an impeccable, dignified image. Be realistic."

"I know that, Larry, but this girl is exquisite. She has incredible charisma. She literally stops traffic. I saw it happen with my own eyes. Beautiful and a top athlete. *And* she's the Symphony's First Chair Flutist. Do you have any idea of how fine a musician you have to be to hold *that* position in *that* orchestra? Couldn't be a better story." A strident pitch overtakes him. "She has star quality. She's a winner. I can *see* it. She *is* Miss Philharmonic. Look, I'll send pictures over to you I took of her in the park. You'll see what I mean."

"Wait a minute," says Larry, "Now you sound like me. You're usually the sensitive guy behind the camera. You hardly talk to women anymore, remember? What's with you?"

"I'm just trying to help."

"Sure you are. Listen, Warren, I know you too well. What's the story?"

Warren tells him about Leslie, about seeing her running, about the scene in the park with the masher and about the cop. "I'd like to get to know her. I figure a photo shoot in my studio would be the perfect place."

"Ah, now I get it. Why didn't you tell me? I know who she is. Beautiful, alright. Everyone in the orchestra seems to love her. And it's about time you started dating again. After that bitch you were married to and all the shit she put you through, hell ... she sure turned out to be a monster. You haven't been the same since."

"I know. I was pretty shattered. Her cleaning out the bank accounts on top of everything else didn't help. But it wasn't the money; I trusted her. I just lost confidence in my judgment and in women. But maybe I'm through it now."

"Well, I'm glad you've finally turned the corner. Tell you the truth, man, I was getting tired of trying to fix you up."

"I'm not talking about just dating. It's more than that. She's special."

"But if you've already spoken to her outside the park and you have her name, why don't you just call her? Why do you need the studio? Seems to me the ice is already broken."

"Talking with her that day may have been a fluke. I didn't have a chance to even think about it. I don't want to freeze up when I talk with her again. I could. But I think I'll be fine in the studio."

"Warren, does she know anything about you? Award winning photographer, Pulitzer nomination, divorced from a witch. All-around good guy? All that stuff?"

"No, nothing. I hardly just met her."

"Well, dude, I've known you for fifteen years and I've never heard you sound so determined. The time must be right for you. She sure has made an impression."

"Yeah, I guess."

"Well, no problem. I'll arrange it … gladly. She should be real happy to get to know you. I'll bring her over to your studio next week. Take a few pictures. Whatever."

"Thanks, man. And Larry, make out like it's your idea. okay?"

"Sure."

The next morning Warren showers and grooms himself carefully, inspecting his hair, his ears, his nose. He stands in front of the mirror, practicing his smile and the words he will say to Leslie. His rehearsal is eloquent and surprisingly forthcoming. He speaks his heart, unwavering and true. The timing is right.

A week later Larry arrives at the studio. "Warren, this is Leslie, the principal flutist with the National Philharmonic. *I was telling you about her?* Oh, that's right you've already met. I forgot. Anyway, as I was saying, I'd like you to do a photo shoot of Leslie, all the glamour stuff, for a possible promotion for the Symphony."

Warren stares at them. He knew they were coming, but he's not ready for her. He's had too much time to think about it. "Oh my, there *is* a God," Warren moans under his breath. He is in shock.

"Excuse me?" says Larry.

"Oh, nothing. Just mumbling to myself. Please come in." She's even more astonishing today. *Look at those lovely long lashes, the insistent blue eyes. She radiates poise, natural dignity.* His insides shiver. He can't understand his feelings. She looks so much more desirable here in the intimacy of his studio.

She carries her flute case and has a light wardrobe bag over her arm. "Pleasure to see you again, Warren."

"Oh, and it's nice to see you, Leslie. The back is in the dressing room. I mean the dressing room is in the back."

"Thank you, Warren," she says, smiling right into his eyes. He is mush now. She appears confident and unaffected. In the park he had admired both her courage and her humor when confronted with the masher. Afterwards on the sidewalk her ease in talking with him and her spunk with the cop impressed him, too. But now, up close in his studio, she floors him.

Larry says goodbye with an aside to Warren, "Good luck, buddy."

In just a few minutes Leslie emerges from the dressing room in a stunning, classic black velour evening dress, single-strap, full length, bare-shouldered. There is a slit on one side, the terminus of which is somewhere well above the knee of an incredibly smooth leg. Oh my, he thinks and sucks in a breath. Around her neck pearls gleam on a single strand and seem to kiss her. He is jealous, sick with desire. He wants to reach out and touch her all over. He can almost feel her softness. His hands perspire. He begins to sweat. His throat dries.

"How does this look, Warren?" she asks.

At that moment his mind decides, without any direction from him, to replay the scene of her running in the park when she had so artfully dispatched the Big Galoot. He blurts out, "You go girl!"

She giggles and says sweetly, "Why, thank you, Warren." He gulps. There isn't anything else he can bring himself to say at the moment. He resolves to ask her out as soon as the photo shoot is over. Just not yet.

He decides to pose Leslie smiling demurely, which she is very good at, looking sexy, which she handles very well, and holding her flute sensuously—sensitively, that is.

"Now, Leslie, let's set up for more shots in a different dress." As he says this, completely in charge, he spills his coffee on his blue shirt. He tries to brush it off with his hand. "Oops. Can't get good help these days. Heh, heh."

She smiles and goes into the dressing area to change.

Why is he so damn nervous? He's photographed hundreds of women and never had this problem in his own studio. Maybe he never cared about any of them. He'll take a few deep breaths. That ought to help.

She returns in a fitted red cocktail dress ennobled with a delicately scooped lace bodice and a scalloped hem. He is shaken.

His confidence returns the moment he holds the camera again. With each terrific shot of Leslie his fine eye captures living art, taking over eighty shots. Even before he asks, she assumes each new pose perfectly with the experience of a professional model. The shoot wraps in two hours.

Time runs out much too quickly for him. All business. No small talk. No chitchat.

I'll open up and talk to her after she changes. Maybe I should casually walk into the dressing room now. I'll say, Excuse me … just have to get some equipment. I can just imagine how she'll be there, nude, so smooth, glowing, so perfect. She'll be standing without shame. Our eyes will lock. Then maybe we'll kiss. Or something.

He can almost feel her naked body against him. He savors the sensation. His heart thumps until conscience snaps him out of his fantasy and rants *What the hell's wrong with you, Warren? You nuts or something? Get real. Wait till she finishes dressing. When she comes out, ask her to lunch. That's the proper way to do it.* Right, he thinks, repentant. I'll wait till she comes out. But what if she says no?

Just ask her. You're nuts about her. She's here. Now ask her. She wants you to.

Leslie steps out of the dressing area in her street clothes, flips her hair back then brushes it to one side with her hand. She seems to be aware that Warren is watching her intently. But how could he not? She looks at Warren with soft eyes.

"Well, thank you, Warren. Today has been a pleasure. By the way, I'm sorry I was so short with you outside the park. I really had to go. But it was great how you spoke up to that cop. And taking those shots was really something."

Now, Warren. Ask her now. Just speak. Come on. You can do it.

"I just happened to be there (pause). Do you think we could, a ... I mean, maybe you'd like to ..."

"Yes?"

"Ahem." He clears his throat.

"Yes, Warren?"

The soles of his feet are warm. He shifts his weight back and forth. He faces her, almost desperately. "Ah, a, oh nothing. Look, thank you for coming."

"Goodbye then, I guess." She holds out her hand. He clasps it with both hands. At once he is electrified by her touch. It exceeds all expectation. His body quivers, almost unbearably.

He releases her hand, opens the door.

She stops. "Warren," she kisses his cheek lightly. "Thank you for today and for almost saving me in the park."

He watches as she walks out to the sidewalk where she hesitates for a moment then turns toward the subway entrance, her soft tresses trailing in the breeze. *Go after her, man. Now. Run. Come on.*

Warren watches as she disappears down the subway stairs. He stands there for a few minutes, staring at the lasting impression of her, an image no one else sees.

He blew it and he knows it. He feels suicidal.

The next afternoon he returns to his studio. He enters slowly, locks the door behind him and walks back toward the utility storage room. On the way, he lingers at the photo shoot set-up, straightens a chair, re-adjusts the light stands. Brushing aside the curtain, he enters the dressing area, closes his eyes, breathes in yesterday. *Oh, the smell of her—clean as the cleanest breeze intoxicated by the purest rose.*

Passing into the storage room, once a darkroom, he absent-mindedly flips on a seldom-used red work light. Awash in the crimson quiet, he fusses aimlessly with old prints and negatives, like an apparition rummaging an attic. He studies an idle developer tray where he used to dab prints in fixative solution before he went digital. He likes to hold onto things of the past. Maybe too much, he thinks. He stands at the workbench, stares, listens to the infinite sound of silence, a distant, high-pitched ringing in his ears, as if millions of miniscule tingling molecules were swirling in the air. He reaches to a shelf, turns on an old developer timer. It pulses with the beat of an obedient metronome. The ticking soothes him. He resigns himself to the comfort of an old easy chair. Today becomes yesterday.

Outside, the late afternoon rush hour is overtaking the city. Buses arc to corner stops, disgorging, then boarding, passengers. Cabs dart for opportunities into open seams looking for quick getaways.

41

Horns beep and blare. A steady flow of determined bodies converges at subway entrances. Silent, except for the Babel-like fugue of shoe-scuffing, they pour down the stairs. Steps quicken at the bottom; feet scurry to get the next Uptown or Downtown train. Tomorrow will be the same.

Sounds of a city-in-a-hurry filter into the front of the closed photography studio. In the quiet of the backroom the timer ticks, tolling the loneliness of yet another hour. Warren's thoughts gradually subdue the rhythmic clicks, until at last the beat is swallowed by silence. His eyes close. His chin finds rest on his chest. He heaves a deep breath. He sees her running by the lake so elegantly. Children are following her. She stops to dispatch the big galoot, turning over his canoe. Holding a paddle, she poses for the photo shoot in a red bathing suit, trying her best to encourage Warren. Now the big galoot is standing waist deep in the water, dripping and cursing. He yells out to Warren *Why didn't you ask her out when she was in your studio? You jerk. He scolds and scowls.*

Well, I spilled the coffee on my shirt, see… and…

When he wakes, he feels exhausted. He yawns, stretches, takes a deep breath. Exhales slowly. Why couldn't he talk to her yesterday? He reasons it just wasn't meant to be. He knows he certainly would have said something if it were right. Just as well. Maybe he's too old for her. But the past three years being alone have been no picnic. Does he want to continue on like that?

Faint Heart Ne'er Won Fair Maid. The saying resonates. Yeah, sure, he knows that. That's no surprise. He was such an insipid dolt yesterday. And he got what he deserved ... nothing. What did he think would happen? She'd ask *him* for a date?

He knows if he could just once ask her out, the ice would be broken. He's got to do it now. How many chances do you get to make a first impression? He wonders if she'll even speak to him after he acted like such a nerd-freak. Okay. But he needs an excuse. The proofs.

He picks up the phone. Puts it down. Picks it up again, dials. It rings "Hello, Leslie? This is Warren." (pause) His breathing is short. "Oh, it was my pleasure, Leslie. I think they'll come out great." (pause) "Sure you can, soon as I print them up." (pause) "Well, it was delightful working with you, too." (This is going better than he expected.) "I was wondering if maybe we could have dinner some night. The proof sheets are ready. We can talk over the shoot and stuff. I could bring them with me. You know, maybe to some nice quiet restaurant, just the two of us?"

His heart thumps like an out-of-sync truck motor. He holds the phone at arm's length, grimaces in anticipation of rejection. (pause) "Tomorrow night? Tomorrow would be great. You're on 83rd, right? Seven good for you?" (pause) "Eight? Eight's even better." (He dances in place, so elated he could run a ten-miler.) "Great. See you tomorrow night around eight, then." (lengthy pause) "What? Do I mind if your roommate comes along?"

Warren sinks. *She's giving me a message. Just being polite. Trying to let me down easy.* "Ah, well, okay, I guess, but ... wait a minute, Leslie. I do mind. I want very much to see you. But I'd like to talk with you alone.

Would you mind telling your roommate 'Not this time'? Okay? Will you do that?" (long pause, silence) "Leslie?"

He may have lost her. Was he too pushy? It's times like this a man just doesn't know what to do. It's all in the hands of the woman.

"Warren," she says in a soft voice, "I don't have a roommate."

"Huh?"

"Larry Bishop told me all about you before I came to your studio. You're a such nice guy. And you've been so considerate of me. I know you're kind of shy, but you didn't really *say* anything to me at your studio. You know, anything of importance. I guess I just needed to see how you'd react to the roommate thing. Kind of far out, huh? Do you mind?"

Relieved, "No. I absolutely understand."

"Good, I'm really glad. By the way, Warren," her voice lightens, "Larry showed me the *rest* of the pictures you took of me earlier in the park. Very interesting. Should I have reported a *stalker* to the cop, too? I think maybe you owe me an explanation."

Gulp.

**

The Hike...

New Hampshire Cure_____

The late May morning broke clear and crisp.
Not a trace of a cloud to feather even a wisp of white
against the blue sky. Perfect. If all went as she planned,
Alison believed the day could change everything. She
needed it to.

"What a beautiful day," she announced with
enough zest to make the spring buds want to bloom
right then.

"That's nice," Barbara ho-hummed, looking up,
interrupting her conversation with Sally.

"Oh yeah, right," Sally added, still half asleep,
ostensibly bored.

Alison had checked the weather forecast. Clear
skies, temperatures somewhat cooler than normal, less
than a ten percent chance of shower activity. Wonderful,
she concluded, with her usual trust in nature, it's an
ideal day for hiking the mountain. She didn't want to

impose on her sisters, but she was certain they would love it when they got to the top, just as she had done once before. Then they would understand her far better. And that was most important to her.

"Isn't this great," Alison announced, already enjoying the bracing fresh air as they set out on the path.

"Oh right," Barbara said, interrupting small-talk with Sally.

"Sure is, honey, you bet," quipped Sally.

They'll catch on soon, thought Alison. She strode ahead confidently, optimistically, certain the hike would work its magic on them and accomplish all she hoped for. The weather indeed looked good. They had packed lunches in knapsacks, had sweaters and jackets and their mood was lighthearted.

Alison had persuaded her sisters to hike the mountain by appealing to their sense of sisterhood and adventure. "After all, it's the last time we'll ever come here, now that were selling the place. It's the only chance we'll ever have to do this together. Think of how much fun it will be. We really ought to do it. It'll be easy."

Her sisters accepted her invitation but received it with expressions of somewhat less than thrall. They shrugged acquiescence, apparently to humor her, accompanied by long looks at each other. Just yesterday she overheard them discussing her idea. "Yeah, the hike thing is okay with me, I guess," said Sally, "but I have my doubts, Barb. You know how spacey Alison can be."

Alison wasn't offended. She understood their hesitation. They were city women. They didn't hike mountains, even a small one like this. A play, a concert or dinner out? Sure. But hike? Hardly.

She had just turned thirty-six, the middle sister of the three. She knew they still regarded her as a dreamer with an active imagination. Which was precisely her point: they didn't comprehend the fact that Mother Nature was the ultimate illusionist, if only one took the time to notice. The logic of her plan did not seem far-fetched to her and she was determined to make the most of the opportunity.

When Alison hiked to the summit before, she felt she could almost touch the sky. She was stunned by the feeling and still remembered it. Looking off in the distance, she had seen the curving stream far below, flowing through the valley floor, a still, serpentine boundary between two vast meadows.

Tall pine trees covered much of the mountain terrain. The way they rustled with optimism in the invisible wind intrigued her. From a distance they were like massive formations of uniformed soldiers to her, marching down the hill, getting taller the closer they got to the base of the mountain. Surreal Roman Legions, majestic, powerful, invincible, they coursed down the slopes into the valley, helmets topped with plumes of new foliage. Once at the bottom, the troops fanned out and dispersed, as if by some magic command, into fields of grass and patches of wild flowers, leaving only diminished traces of forest.

Their widowed father's gruffness hadn't prevented Alison from maintaining contact with him. "Yes, Dad, I'll come up to visit you next weekend." Because she lived closest to him after her two sisters had moved far away, she felt responsible to make monthly weekend trips from Boston to New Hampshire to check on him.

There was little reward in this, except in doing what she considered her duty.

She had to endure the brunt of her father's irascibility. He didn't hesitate to try to provoke her.

"Still teaching that stupid art stuff at that little college?"

"Yes, Dad, of course. You ask me that every time I come to see you."

"Why don't you get married and forget that crap?"

"Dad, you don't understand. I love what I do, and I'm good at it."

"Seems like a crock, a hellava waste of time."

Her visits to his New Hampshire cabin continued until he died because she knew he needed company. At some point when their visits became unpleasant— invariably they did—she would deflect his insensitivity by imagining the solace of being on the mountain.

How incredible, Alison often mused, that such a mountain could have formed over fifteen thousand years ago, the ice-carved product of the dredge and drag of an ice age. How glorious. With all the amazing things man has built, making a mountain was far beyond his capabilities. But then, why would he want to anyway? Nature had done it so perfectly.

From the time the three first decided to meet for their reunion at their deceased father's cabin, Alison began thinking of hiking the mountain together. If only they could experience what she had felt at the summit, not only would they most certainly understand her better, they would also experience a sense of accomplishment that would rekindle camaraderie, giving them new pride in their sisterhood. In doing so, they would discover a different reality, one far removed from their spheres of city life. Climbing a mountain together, a modest one, true, would be a first-time feat, the memory of which they'd always share.

Barbara, 40, the oldest, divorced her husband a few years ago after discovering the back seat of their van was being used as an audition couch for cocktail waitresses.

Alison had said to her at the time, "Don't you think divorce is a little severe, Barb? Maybe the marriage can be saved."

"Listen, it wasn't the first time. I should have paid more attention when I noticed his eye contact with certain waitresses, like mental infidelities. It galled me. Later I just found out the truth, that's all. You can't trust them. Their crotch leads them around like dogs. They can't help them themselves. So watch out, girls, if they get too friendly with waitresses," she added with a laugh. "They might be telling you something."

Alison offered no other comment, but joined in with Sally, sympathizing with the usual 'that rodent' observations shared by the world's sisterhood in times of betrayal. Privately Alison wondered why Barbara didn't seem more affected by what happened to her marriage, dealing with it almost pragmatically.

Barbara was the one who had been estranged from their father, yet never discussed it with them, at least not with Alison. She didn't even attend his funeral last year. When Alison asked if she were coming, Barbara replied, "NO!" Alison never questioned her older sister, but often wondered what happened between her and their father. She concluded she'd never know.

Alison admired her sisters. They seemed to be able to handle adversity with a minimum of emotional upheaval, making decisions, getting on with their lives, not dwelling on things. She, on the other hand, still tried to revise the past and put people into more pleasant pictures. If that didn't work, she'd immerse herself in nature and art to ponder and create her own interpretations of reality.

After an hour walking the path on the lower mountain, the rise of the incline increased noticeably. Each step took a little more energy. Their pace slowed.

"How much farther Ali?" questioned Sally.

"Oh, it's less than two hours from here to the top and the views are extraordinary. You'll love it."

"Hmm. Two more hours, huh." It wasn't a question.

"Maybe less," Alison said, as she took note of a few clouds moving in. But it didn't concern her much. The weather forecast had been positive. They continued the upward trek.

Sassy Sally, as her friends called her, the youngest of the sisters, plied a fairly successful TV career working small parts in various Soaps in Los Angeles. She had never been known for her shyness. In fact, her reputation for being direct was legend among family and friends. She had a no-nonsense way of putting things succinctly, even with strangers. Alison envied that. Answering a telemarketer's call she might say, "What the hell do I want another credit card for? You leeches want my blood, too? Don't call me again."

An hour later the weather changed. Mist began to move onto the mountain, and with it came an insistent drizzle. Alison looked for a break in the overcast. Didn't see any. The weather quickly became soupy. She had to face the fact that nature was taking charge, as it sometimes did. And, as if the morbid drizzle weren't enough, the temperature was dropping dramatically. She could feel it. Ordinarily she wouldn't care. Now she felt betrayed. Why today of all days?

At this point she thought about turning back. But they had already come two-thirds of the way to the top. It would be a shame to give up now. The weather could clear just as suddenly as it fouled. Maybe it would. She kept leading up the trail.

The mist shrouded heavier and colder and at length settled in around them, fogging their breath, enveloping the path—distorting visibility into almost unnatural impressions, trees like apparitions, boulders like shadows, shrubs a few feet from the path fading into fog. Sally and Barbara seemed stunned by what was happening.

Yet for Alison, even in the wet and cold, it was a mystical experience. She halted abruptly, looked into the surrounding woods and gestured with outstretched arms.

"What?" said a startled Sally. "What is it? What do you see?"

"Look at the trees, Alison said, almost whispering. "See how stoic? How proud. They just stand there, watching. They see it all, no matter what, rain, lightning, snow, people, animals. They're impervious, implacable. They don't worry. They just are. We could learn from them."

"For God's sakes, said Sally with a scowl, "screw the trees. I'm getting soaked!"

"Me too," Barbara said. "What's with you, Ali?"

"Oh, nothing. Just a thought I had. Never mind."

Her sisters looked at each other, rolled their eyes, and swayed their heads. If she were hiking alone, Alison would have dawdled and studied the dripping trailside giants, fantasizing they were observing her. She knew it was a harmless quirk of hers, a what-if game she sometimes played with her art students at Emerson College.

"Use your imagination, she often advised them. Don't assume trees are merely inanimate life," pointing to the oaks and willows on Boston Common near the Swan Boats. "Look carefully at them. Really see them. What if they could speak? What would they say? Get inside of them. Sketch what's there. Make your drawing live. Feel what the tree feels. There's more to nature than what you think you see."

"Are you teaching college art or Zen?" her friend Chris once asked her.

"They're pretty much the same," she said.

A trailside sign read El.1800. "Hmm, grunted Sally." It could just as well have read El. 18,000 given the weather. Obviously, their mood had soured. Alison couldn't blame them. She began to feel guilty. A chill began to rake her back. Her thumbs met the tips of her fingers, rolling back and forth over them, working them like prayer beads. Her long brown tresses, matted from the drizzle, trailed out from under her Red Sox cap and clung to her jacket. The weather had definitely deteriorated and she feared the worst. Her plan might backfire.

"Ali, don't you think we should be heading back?" Barbara said. "Its pretty yucky and I think I've had it." Her knitted hat was soaked. Its tassel hung down onto the collar of her windbreaker, covering her Save The Symphony pin.

"Right," announced Sally, mopping her face with her sleeve. "Look, I'm drenched. That's it for me. We should go back NOW."

"We could do that," Alison said, trying desperately to salvage the adventure. "But there's a hikers shelter up ahead just a couple of minutes. When we get to it, we can rest, dry off, have a snack, and wait till the weather clears. Then maybe we can go to the top."

"Are you saying it'll clear?" Sally challenged. Her tone bore the edge of a dagger.

"Sometimes this stuff moves in on the mountain then all of a sudden just blows away. If it does, we'll go on. If it doesn't, we'll head back. Okay?" Alison kept her voice light and cheery, like their Mother's sounded when giving them a spoonful of cod liver oil when they were kids. 'Sunshine', their mother called it. They hated it.

"Okay," said Barbara, "but only a few minutes more."

Sally piped up, "Let's try not to get any wetter than fish, for Gods sake. And I've got to rest soon. I'm tired."

The spring grass stubble they had seen poking through the soggy turf on the lower hills an hour before was now checkered with patches of leftover snow. Alison knew the trail was too sloppy to continue, even for someone as lean and fit as she, but still she hoped they would make it to the top.

By the time they reached the shelter, the wind had picked up, whining through the trees like a witch, bending and whipping branches. May became December.

The shelter had three walls of logs resting on a raised wood-plank floor. The flat roof slanted up toward the open side, confronting the mountain trail. The closed back of the shelter faced the valley. There were no windows. Wide benches lined the three walls. There was space to stand up, except near the entrance where the roof overhang extended down a foot to protect against weather. It was a typical State Forestry shelter.

They stumbled in, lips pursed, brushing off the wet, looking grim. With her backpack on, Sally plopped herself down on a bench, the heaviness of the pack pulling her like workout weights. She leaned back against the wall, legs splayed, eyes shut.

Barbara took off her pack, carefully placed it on a bench, sat next to it, dried her face with paper towels she had packed and said, "Some walk in the park, huh?"

"At least this gives us a chance to be together." Alison said, doing her best to change their focus with the kind of cozy goodie remark the girls had expected of her over the years.

"Yeah, sure," quipped Sally, having none of it. "I haven't had this much fun since my cat died. This sucks."

"Oh come on, Sally," said Barbara, recovering a bit of her big sister demeanor, "it's an adventure. You'd probably be acting for free with some LA street-corner Shakespeare group if you weren't here this week. I know how you audience-hungry actresses are."

"At least I wouldn't be freezing," Sally said. "Besides, that trail is slippery as hell. And I'm tired and cold and old."

"You're not old, Sally," countered Alison, trying to make nice. "Thirty-two isn't old. Besides, you used to be an ice skater when you were a kid. Just imagine you're skating."

"Ice skating is flat, honey. Not up hill."

Alison smiled tightly. "Why don't you two get out the snacks and rest a while. I'm going outside behind the shelter to see if the valley shows any signs of clearing, so we can decide what to do. I'll be back in a few minutes." She took a poncho out of her pack, slipped her head though the center slit. She should have done this before, she knew, but they had seemed too tired to stop. She stooped under the roof overhang and disappeared into the driving rain.

Rivulets of water ran down the trail from above, splashing mini dams of pine needles at her feet like. How intriguing, she reflected, and picked her way around to the back of the shelter. Blanketed by dense clouds the valley was invisible. *Damn.* Carefully, she stepped down the trail a little farther testing the footing. She stood there for a few minutes trying to decide what to do then worked her way back to the shelter. She was just about to enter when she overheard her sisters talking. She stopped to listen.

Barbara was speaking, apparently munching on some food. "Sure, but don't you think you're being a little rough on Ali?" She stopped for a moment, as if swallowing. "So this was her idea, right. But you know how sensitive she is. I'm sure she feels worse about this than we do."

"Oh yeah? I'm not so sure about that," Sally said. "She doesn't think ahead and now she's got us into a mess. And since when did you get so compassionate?"

"Boy, you're bitchy today. What's with you?"

"I'm pregnant."

"You're what?"

"Pregnant. As in soon to be a fatso."

"My God, Sally. Who's the father?"

"A guy I know in LA. Who cares?"

"How far along are you?"

"Seven weeks."

"You're not showing."

"I am on the inside."

"Why didn't you tell us before? This is serious. You shouldn't be hiking a mountain in your condition, especially on a day like this."

"Who knew? I thought I could do it. I'm in good shape. Besides, I couldn't very well can the hike, could I? Not with the bonding-bash-of-the-decade at stake. Listen, I know how Alison feels about this sort of stuff. I just didn't want to disappoint her."

"Jeez," said Barbara. "So we haven't been together in couple of years, but really, Sally ..."

Alison emerged through the wall of rain, flailing her arms back and forth across her chest. "I'm hungry," she said, noticing the sandwiches. "It's getting colder. Bundle up. Looks like well be here a while."

"Ali," Barbara announced, "Sally is seven weeks pregnant."

"I know, I just overheard. Congratulations, Sally," she said, as sweetly as she could manage. "Why didn't you tell us?"

"I just did." "How do you feel?"

"Not good. Borderline lousy. In fact, forget borderline. I just crossed the border. The last part of the climb did it. And this is a climb, honey!"

"Calm down," said Barbara.

"I am calm!"

"Well, there's no way we should go up any farther, even if it clears," Alison said.

"Good," said Sally. "Let's get dry."

The gray look on Alison's face said it all. She knew her well-intended plan was finished and that the day was only worsening her relationship with her sisters. Swallowing her disappointment she said, "You should lie down on the bench, Sally. Here, put my pack under your knees. You need to rest."

Sally didn't move. She was staring open-mouthed at the exposed side of the shelter. "What the hell is that?"

The other two turned around. "It's snow!" said Barbara. "But it's May! Give me a break. Ali? What the hell?"

"Yes, I can see it," said Alison quietly. "It's snow."

"Dammit. We should go down now."

"We can't. Too slippery," said Alison, again quietly.

"Shit," responded Sally.

"Come on, Sally, lie down," Alison mothered. "Get your feet up. Don't worry. We'll figure something out. I'll get you down."

"You'll get us down? Hmm. Well, there's one way to get me down. Put me on that trail on my back. I'll slide down like a porpoise. I feel like one."

Barbara couldn't contain it and burst out laughing. Alison made an effort not to giggle. "Oh, Sally, you're too much."

At first they didn't notice the large black bear just outside the shelter, grunting in the snow. It stood there like a snow-specked steamer trunk on four hairy posts. Scraggly, wet, bow-legged, swinging its head side to side, it raised its snout and sniffed, then stared at them as if it owned the mountain and was there to collect the rent.

"Oh my God," Barbara gasped, dropping her sandwich.

"Holy shit," said Sally. "What'll we do? What'll we do?"

"Don't panic," said Alison calmly. She really didn't know what to do, having never confronted a bear, but she knew it was up to her to think of something. "Push your backpacks away from you slowly. Don't look him in the eye. Easy. No sudden moves. Lie down quietly on the benches. Curl up. Quick. Cover your heads."

"What for?" said Barbara, as if an oldest sister should be in charge.

"Do it now, Alison ordered. "Cover your head with your arms. Face the wall. Now!" she whispered. "Don't move no matter what happens. It's probably just looking for food. We'll let him have it. And stay still."

"The bear glared as they assumed fetal positions. Then it swaggered in like a fat, drunken general. The women squeezed their eyes shut. They could smell the animal stinking like a sewer and heard its claws clacking across the floor. It seemed to be in no hurry as it followed its nose, finding food, tearing at backpacks, grunting and ripping them apart, devouring anything edible.

When it finished with the backpacks, the bear came up over Sally and sniffed at the ketchup spilled on her windbreaker. A heavy paw poked at it, tearing part of the garment away. Miraculously the swipe missed Sally, now rigid as a petrified rock. The bear moved away.

As it approached Barbara she turned outward and started kicking at it. "Get away from me, you bastard! Get off me. Get off me. Let me alone!"

Her cry resonated in Alison. She vaguely remembered hearing words like that late at night many years ago. In that instant she understood Barbara's refusal to attend their father's funeral.

"No Barb, don't do that! Get down," she warned.

The bear hovered closer. Alison watched as Barbara swung her head side to side, trying to avoid the agitated bear. A giant paw swatted at Barbara's knitted stocking cap that was flipping back and forth, and tore it from her head just as she turned away. She screamed then rolled down onto the bench, moaning in pain.

The bear poked at her, growling with agitation.

"Bastard," she whimpered.

"Barbara, cover up!" Alison yelled. Then without waiting another second, she jumped up and bolted out of the shelter making as much noise and commotion as she could. "Yah, Yah, Hey, Hah, Yea, Yea, Hah!" She yelled and bellowed as she ran up the slippery trail, pushing ahead with all her strength. The bear swung around and clumped after her. She had about a fifteen-yard head start. She reached into her pocket as she ran, and pulled out a whistle, blowing it loudly over and over. The bear quickly gained on her.

Cornered, she braced her back against a thin birch just off the trail and blew the whistle furiously. She knew better than to make eye contact with the bear, avoiding the challenge it would instinctively accept. The shrill blasts shrieked against the trees and rocks, resounding through the woods. The bear slowed, then stopped only a few feet from her. It growled, raised up, bared its gums, showed its teeth, sniffed the air, making long hissing sounds, the way bears do when withdrawing from a fight. It swayed, sniffed again, then rumbled off into the woods, leaving its odor to nuance the essences of the fresh snow. Alison kept blowing the whistle.

When she thought it had gone, she ran back to the shelter and found Barbara sitting on the floor shivering in shock. Sally, trembling, said, "Oh my God, oh my God. Ali, we thought the bear was going to kill you." She had wrapped what was left of her torn windbreaker around Barbara's head.

"It's over. He's gone. Let me take a look, Barb." Alison uncovered her sister's head and saw the injury was not serious. The bear had barely grazed her. Another miracle. The bleeding was minor, but Barbara was white with shock. Using their first aid kit Alison cleaned the wound, applied a compress bandage and re-wrapped Barbara's head. Then she took off her own sweater, shouldered it around her older sister, and with a maternal hug said, "Barb, you're going to be fine. The bleeding's almost stopped already. Really. Don't worry. We'll get through this together."

Barbara responded with a little smile and a submissive, "Thank you, Ali."

Turning toward her younger sister, Alison said, "You all right, Sally?"

"He, he didn't hurt me," she said, shivering and stunned. "I, I guess Big Bubba prefers older women," nodding toward Barbara.

Barbara turned her head slowly and stuck out her tongue at Sally. Sally returned the gesture. Alison shook her head, admiring her sisters' spunk. No hysterics. No tears.

The blinding snow stopped abruptly, as if canceled by a curtain slamming down during a performance. The sun broke though the detaching clouds and immediately began to beam the chill off the mountain.

"Oh my God, it's over," celebrated Sally. "It stopped snowing! It stopped snowing! The three sisters stared out of the shelter with the unison of a silent choir.

Sally looked at Alison. "Ali, thank God you're okay. I can't believe you did that. You could have been killed. You saved us. I mean, you really saved us. You're frigging amazing. I mean it. I never thought that you ..."

Barbara interrupted. "My God, Ali, you have amazing courage. You're some kind of a rock. Thank you. You surely did save us. I'm so proud of you, sis."

"Will the bear come back, Ali?" asked Sally, with new-found humility.

"I don't think so. But we better start down the trail now, though. Leave the food here. You know, just in case. Funny, they've always said there were no bears on this mountain I've never heard of one here. Besides, black bears aren't supposed to behave like grizzlies except maybe in the movies."

They were quiet. Alison's wistful look showed she knew how lucky they had been.

"Movies? Oh, yeah?" Sally said, suddenly perking up. "Well, this sure would make one hellava flick. And since I'm the only professional, I should get top billing. I can just see the Previews now: *PREGNANT SALLY FIGHTS OFF GIGANTIC BEAST* (growls, snarls) *SAVES*

HIKERS. *Sisters Help a Little*. Huh? Huh?" They laughed together. No need to talk it all out now, sister to sister. The deed had done what words could not.

As Alison watched her sisters get their things together, she remembered scenes from years ago, little kids playing in their backyard in Greenfield, Massachusetts. Sassy Sally at four, banging on the door of their life-size, yellow dollhouse with white trim, calling out to its imaginary old-crag inhabitant, 'Let me in, let me in, or I'll puff your stupid house down!' On the steps of the back porch eleven-year-old Barbara sits comparing dolls with a girlfriend. Eight-year-old Alison holds her favorite stuffed toy lion, engaged in an animated three-way conversation with the hollyhocks.

The flashback vanished as quickly as it appeared. Alison refocused. Why does life have to change? Why couldn't they play in the backyard of their minds with favorite toys and subtle joys forever? It was as if the clock had whirled ahead from those early days to this moment without stopping.

Alison was shivering now, but not because of the cold. Looking at her sisters, an eerie sensation gripped her. Her body was shaking. Emotions brimmed at her control. Struggling to maintain, feigning a cough, hand to face, she backed out of the shelter, turned and slipped into the nearby woods. She couldn't let her sisters see her like this. Not now. Not today. Not ever.

Alone, Alison gave the moment its due. She leaned against a large poplar and let the tears flood until her shaking eventually ebbed to a halt. No need to explain.

The tree understood. She watched the sun reach though the bare branches with new hope.

**

Trapped...
*Buried Below*_____

Before rays of the morning sun found the valleys, while the hills still lay lightly laced with overnight frost, the piercing sound of the siren ripped into homes, uninvited, unwanted, barging into dreams, swirling about, making no sense, then roared out into reality.

Sitting in front of the TV news with his first cup of coffee, Jess Carter knew the siren meant only one thing. Immediately he began to suit up, not looking forward to what might be ahead. Within minutes he would be on his way to the mine.

Three years had passed since the siren last shattered the tranquility of this small western Pennsylvania town, signaling a mining accident that took seven lives. Since then, Jess was in the habit of sleeping lightly, expecting at any time to hear the sound that could summon him to the upper reaches of hell.

65

Before the blaring stopped, Jess had already slipped into the light-reflecting coveralls, which had hung on a hook in the kitchen. He wrapped his lip-belt around him, put on steel-toed shoes, and grabbed his air-filtering mask, his boots and 'self-rescuer box'. He secured his safety goggles, an extra battery pack, gloves and hard-hat, quickly stowed everything into his Ford F-150 and high-geared it to Beltson Coal Mine. Minutes later, parking inside the gate, he threw on the rest of his equipment, making his way to the lift, rather than to the main tunnel entrance several hundred yards away. Men gathered around him as he walked.

"Cave in, Jess," yelled one.

"I know."

"You going in?" said another. He didn't answer.

Dirt and smoke still plumed up the open elevator shaft. He stepped into the cage, put on his mask and pressed the green button. With a lurch the open car clanked down the spine of the mine. The farther down it went the more the whooping of arriving emergency vehicles on the surface faded. Soon he became immersed in quiet, except for the eerie screech of metal and cables carrying him deeper and darker.

If men were trapped, he would do all he could to prevent the dreaded blank looks of despair from masking the faces of potential new widows. Jess knew what it was like to grow up without a father. He had chosen not to marry and have a family of his own.

Words of his mother resonated in his head, spoken to him when he was a boy after tons of the precious black rock had crushed his father, "Jessie, you promise me, right here and now," she said, as if swearing him to an oath, "you'll never become a coal miner." He had kept his word. Yet here he was, a rescuer.

At the bottom of the shaft, where the lift intersected with the main tunnel, he began the slow trek toward the accident site. Black air billowed and bulged at him, slapping against his mask, plunging past, finding escape up the elevator shaft. His helmet light burrowed a surreal tube through the thick dust, penetrating not more than a yard in front of him.

He pushed forward, down the slopping main tunnel, gingerly managing his footing.

The mile-long shaft angled down to a point well past the 1,000-foot level. Aware that toxic gases often seep from coal when it is cut free, Jess knew that cave-ins can release an invisible volatile mass easily hair-triggered into a lethal explosion. Carrying a portable telephone and a methane gas-detecting Davy safety lamp, he had no idea how much gas had escaped this time; but it was his job to find out.

To a stranger unfamiliar with a miner's safety gear, he might have looked like an underground version of an astronaut. Jess kept his gas detection meter close to his face, watching it. So far readings did not come close to crossing into the red zone. A good sign.

The same mine had swallowed his father years ago, along with thirty-six other men, when methane gas exploded deep below the surface striking like a petulant monster with an unpredictable appetite.

Despite the inevitability of such disasters, miners continued to deliver themselves into the belly of the earth, scraping, chipping, drilling and blasting at its innards for the valuable lining hoarded there, never knowing when the angry Grendal-like demon would clamp its jaws shut again, crushing its prey.

Wives and families waited, hoping for rescues, hating the mine, though knowing that working in its dungeons made it possible for their miners to provide for their families. The pay was high but so were the risks.

Jess Carter resolved to do everything possible to save those trapped in the black hollows. It became his mission in life. He learned all he could about the mine… every artery, every vein, every inch of its clawed-out walls. He knew about methane, carbon monoxide build-up, explosion potential, cave-ins and structural weaknesses, and kept abreast of the latest rescue techniques and technologies.

By forty-five Jess had become the Red Adair of this small western Pennsylvania town, as well as the surrounding areas. Unlike Adair, who was noted for capping out-of-control burning oil wells, rugged Jess had become the go-to man whenever there was a mining emergency. Everyone knew him.

He was the bulldog, the trouble-shooter. His early assessment of damage and subsequent plan were the first steps in rescue attempts.

Jess removed his mask and reported clearance status to the top. No gas. When the smoke lessened at the entrance a rescue team descended and began tracking him through the sloping tunnel. Up top, murmurs of both hope and despair rippled the waiting crowd. A broadcast truck from WTEL-TV had already begun telecasting from the scene.

"How the hell did those TV guys get here so fast?" demanded Lou Lavery, the mine superintendent, after he jammed his pick-up truck to a skidding stop in front of the office and dashed out.

"They didn't," an assistant said excitedly. "They were here before the cave-in."

"What the hell for?"

"The TV news reporter, Carole Peterson, went into the mine an hour ago with a cameraman and some of our guys. Coulter gave them permission to do it. They're working on a documentary about Coal Mining — America's Answer to the Energy Crises. I think they even planned to broadcast from the mine at 8:00AM."

"You can't be serious. And he didn't tell me?"

"I guess he forgot."

"Christ, I guess. Where is he now?"

"Tampa, I think. Deep-sea fishing."

"Where's Jess?"

"Heard from him a while ago him. Said he was down 600 feet, about a half-mile in, past Station Two. He's got a small crew working with him now. The cave-in is at Three North. It's impassable. Three South seems ok. He's coming up now with the guys who were safe. He'll give us a report."

"How many guys are coming up?"

"Sixteen or seventeen."

"Who's with the TV people? They okay?"

"Fergis was escorting them. They were going into the old shaft."

"Three North?"

"Yeah."

"What the hell for?"

"I don't know."

"Oh Jesus, great. The last time Fergis was down more than a hundred feet in a shaft he pissed his pants. Why the hell did *he* go there with them?"

"The boss told him he could. He's the company PR guy, isn't he? Maybe he saw a way to get his face on TV. Make his wife think he's important."

"PR guy, my ass. Fergis is Coulter's stupid son-in-law. You get to do asinine things like that when you're the owner."

Lavery hurried over to the TV truck. "You guys still have a hook-up from your people in the mine?"

"No, nothing. Had a signal for a while. Lost it just after we heard a faint roar, before the smoke and dirt came busting out of the entrance. You know Carole Peterson's down there, don't you?"

"Yeah, we know. We'll do our best to get everyone out."

Some time later the grind of the elevator clanked louder as the open bucket ratcheted to the surface. Jess and several miners, looking like jungle night-fighters — blackened except for the whites of their eye sockets — stepped out.

Wives and families cried with joy as their men moved toward them. Others watched Jess for a sign. He went over to Lavery who was waiting for him and shook his head slowly. Not a good sign. One woman gasped. Another fainted. The crowd hushed.

"How bad is it, Jess?" Lavery asked.

"Best I can tell, five miners and the TV crew are trapped. Don't know if they're alive. Air's ok in the main tunnel. Shoring collapsed in the North Shaft. Probably gas in there. Don't know how much. Soon as we can get a probe through we'll know."

"No explosion?"

"No. Guys in Three South made it out okay. They heard timbers cracking and yelled to the others to run before the ceiling let go. The TV crew and the guys with them didn't get out in time."

"That shaft's supposed to be closed. The shoring wasn't safe to begin with. Why the hell did they go in there?"

"Don't know. Apparently, it wasn't completely sealed off. Somebody screwed up."

"I'll bet it was Fergis, that asshole. How far in are they? How much do we have to dig through to get to them?"

"Hard to say. The cave-in happened near the shaft entrance. They must be at least a hundred feet in, because the guys said they were in pretty far when they yelled to them to take cover. I'm hoping they are. My guess is twenty-five yards or so of blockage, maybe more. There's a sharp turn about 100 feet into the shaft. It might have stopped the collapse from spreading. There's always a chance. We're shoring up now. Our best shot is straight through the debris. I'll need more equipment. I'm going back there now with extra crew." The somber look on Jess's face indicated more, but he said only, "If there's a way to get to them, we will."

Jess knew that even ten yards of fallen timber, rock and coal was impossible to clear quickly. The shaft ceiling was too low for heavy equipment. If they could drill a probe and get a pipe through the blockage with hand-held pneumatic equipment, they might be able to get air to them … if any were still alive. He hoped they had made it to the safety room in time. But he didn't like their chances.

Even if there were no gas build-up yet, he figured they'd have about ten hours of air at most, unless they could get an air pipe through.

The men who escaped told him the TV people weren't completely suited-up or carrying safety equipment, but they did have coveralls on and wore hard hats. At least that was something.

Jess knew of Carole Peterson's intrepid reputation, all 105 pounds of her. He had seen her morning telecasts from mountain tops, open cockpits of airplanes, and from ships tossing about in Nor'easters in the middle of Lake Erie. People like that sometimes have a way of surviving. Jess figured she was a strong woman and hoped she'd have a chance to show her grit this time.

Hardly recognizable, coughing, her face and clothes layered with dirt and coal dust, blonde hair peppered with black specks, Carole Peterson drew herself up from the mine floor. The miners had their hardhat lights on. No one appeared injured. The shaft's string of intermittent bulbs was dark.

"Everybody okay?" asked foreman Morrissey, one of the miners who had accompanied them.

Nods and grunts. "No gas so far. Don't anyone light any matches. We're lucky. Anybody hurt?" More negative grunts. "You okay, Miss Peterson?"

She pulled the hair away from her face and ran a hand through it. "Just another day in Paradise," she said, assessing the situation around her.

"We'll work on the rubble from our side," said Morrissey, as if he hadn't heard her. "They'll have crews working to get us out. We lost phone communication."

"Is the camera all right, Pat?"

"Yeah, Carole. I had it wrapped like a baby in my arms all the time. We're *both* fine, thanks."

Positioning herself in a small clearing, she asked him to get ready to "roll tape".

He switched on the camera light. It immediately illuminated the darkness of the cave like a fun house. Eerie shadows danced the walls, demons elongating and distorting every time the camera moved. He pointed a finger at her to go.

"This is Carole Peterson," she said, looking into to the camera as it taped her, "we're trapped in Beltson Coal Mine near Haversford, Pennsylvania. Eight of us are here. When the ceiling started to collapse the miners in our group yelled for us to follow them. We ran farther into the shaft and dove into a safety room. It's not really a room, just a hollowed-out space cut into the side of the shaft. It wasn't far from the cave-in. It saved our lives. We're all okay."

Dirt fell from overhead. She crouched for a moment then brushed it off without pausing. "Right now the men are ramming some kind of metal probe into the collapsed section to see how thick it is. Pitch black here, except for the camera light and helmet lights. The air is heavy with coal dust.

"We're keeping our noses and mouths covered. Bob Morrissey, one of the miners, says there's no gas escaping so far. Thank God.

"Five miners are here, plus my cameraman, Pat Lennon. Also a Beltson company rep, Albert Fergis, who is not available for comment at the moment. The names of the other miners are, Calvin Herst, Kevin MacKay, Harry Conley and Peter Haase. As I said, we're all okay so far. That's our status. It's scary and dark, but no one is injured. I don't know how long it will take rescuers to reach us. I know they will be trying. Pray for us, folks. Carole Peterson here, somewhere in Hell, signing off, saving our batteries ... and our air. Except for this: *Jess Carte*r, (the camera zoomed in for a close-up) if you're anywhere nearby, I'm hoping you'll get us out of here. If anybody can find a way, I know you will." The camera stopped recording. The light went off.

"Carole, how are we going to get this cassette cartridge up to the broadcast truck?" asked her cameraman.

"Who knows? At least people will know someday what happened here if we don't get out."

"Don't say that!" said Fergis, gray with dirt and debris, huddled in a corner, shivering in his hardhat, blue business suit, brown shoes and white socks. "I shouldn't have come down here. I shouldn't have," he whined.

"Yeah, well you're here," said Morrissey. "Now how about getting off your ass and start helping us. Grab a shovel and start digging."

With the grim, chiseled face of a man who had weathered storms, Jess directed his men, pulling apart debris, cautiously removing beams piece by piece. Care had to be taken to make sure remaining ceiling supports didn't collapse. "Hold up, men," he said. "I don't like it. Shore up again." Dirt sifted from the ceiling. Work stopped. Another crew came forward and began to wedge metal grids against the ceiling with beam supports and jacks to stabilize the old timbers.

Whenever a shim was gently pounded into place with rubber hammers, more dirt fell from above. It took guts to continue, but the men knew what would happen if they were trapped: others wouldn't stop searching for them, no matter how dangerous it was.

Another team set up in the tunnel, preparing piping of various sizes and lengths and larger drill bits to bore through and create a small opening. Superintendent Lavery joined Jess and the team in the staging area. "Got everything you need? Compressor? Drills? Power connections? Enough light?"

"Uh-huh. Pneumatic drills too," said Jess.

"Enough pipe?"

"Plenty. Let's hope we can get through in time. It'll take hours to penetrate. Lots of junk in there."

"Anybody hear anything from the other side?"

"We've had contact mikes on the blockage. Nothing yet. Probably too thick. Nothing on the phones either."

The ABC Television Network interrupted its morning programming to report nationwide. *TV newswoman, Carole Peterson, of ABC affiliate station WTEL, has been reported trapped deep in a western Pennsylvania coal mine along with several miners.*

Thirty-two-year-old Peterson reportedly entered Beltson Mine, near Haversford, Pennsylvania, with a film crew at six-thirty this morning. According to our information, a cave-in apparently occurred about a half hour later. She and several miners have been cut off. Eight people are trapped. Their condition is unknown. Eighteen miners have been taken out safely.

Beltson Mine has claimed the lives of several miners before. Three years ago seven miners were killed. In 1972, thirty-seven were lost in an explosion. Beltson Mine has received several citations from the Bureau of Mines for safety deficiencies. Company officials are not yet available for comment. We will keep you updated with further developments."

A second WTEL-TV remote truck arrived. A camera crew set up on its roof and panned the scene of the company yard as the network announcement was being made.

At home in Aliquippa, Mary Elizabeth Carter heard the broadcast having her morning tea in the kitchen. When the announcement finished she walked into the living room and stood before the empty fireplace. Tears filled her eyes. The handsome, rugged young man in the black and white picture on the wooden mantle smiled at her. Had it really been thirty-eight years since she kissed him goodbye that last morning and held up seven-year-old Jess for a squeeze and a hug from his dad?

Later in the bedroom Mary Elizabeth placed a votive candle into a squat, red glass holder on the dresser top and lit it. The white lace doily underneath bathed in a reflected soft red hue. She watched until she was sure the flame was secure then looked up to the crucifix and prayed.

She sat down on the patched quilt at the end of her bed. Her son would be leading the rescue by now. He had promised her he'd retire from rescuing soon. Fingering her rosary beads, mumbling a mantra of prayers, her gaze was transfixed on the blur of the candle flame. Then she lay on her bed and shut her eyes. The candle would have to carry on.

Pastor McCrae comforted friends and extended family members who had gathered at Haversford's First Baptist Church. The small, wood frame building, painted white inside and out, soon filled with townsfolk.

Vocal strains of *The Old Rugged Cross* and *Amazing Grace* filled the hall and could be heard down the street. People left their homes to gather there and pray for the safe return of those trapped. Businesses closed. At times like these togetherness helped.

In Stamford, Connecticut, Carole Peterson's sister, an account executive for a New York City advertising agency, heard the story on her car radio. She called her office, then the airline, then immediately headed for LaGuardia Airport.

Five hours passed.

Rescue workers continued the struggle to remove debris. Still no indication of gas and no sign of life from the other side of the cave-in. As they drilled carefully, pressurized water was added to keep lethal coal dust fumes from developing.

Five more hours.

More debris and coal removed. Shoring reinforced. Men worked as fast as they could, taking turns in shifts. The staging tunnel was getting muddy. Covered with wet black dust and dirt the men slogged back and forth, farther and farther into the muck to shore timbers, remove debris and man the drills in teams.

Jess was wringing with sweat in the stifling heat. Extraction fans were engaged offering some relief. He hoped the trapped people had air, if they were still alive. If the clock ran out before they could be reached, it wouldn't give them more time, even an extra minute. A buzzer wouldn't sound, sending the game into overtime. The end was the end.

It had been twelve hours since the cave-in. "Come on, guys, push it," Jess said. A rescuer thought he heard a faint tapping from the far side and called out.

Everything stopped. He banged on a metal pipe. All strained to listen. Nothing. Not a sound. Again men picked up their tools to continue.

"Hold it," said Jess, "I heard something. Anybody else?"

"I hear it," said one. "Me too," said another.

The distant sound of three metal-on-metal taps could be heard, repeated over and over.

"Come on, guys," Jess said. "Somebody's home. Tap back three times. Confirm we hear them."

They cheered briefly and banged hard on the fallen debris, three times, then again, then again. As if muted by layers of cotton, five taps came from the other side confirming whoever was there heard the rescue team. "Let's get them, guys!" said Jess. The rescue team stepped up the pace. Jess sent word to the top that they had heard tapping from the other side, faint, but definite. Someone was still alive!

Soon they had drilled enough to get a pipe all the way through. They ran a test line through the tube. No gas. It was clear! At least so far. Amazing, Jess reflected. Given the situation, it seemed like a miracle. They withdrew the line and started pumping air into the tube.

A man's voice yelled, muffled, distant, barely audible, "This is Morrissey. We're all okay. No gas. No injuries. Ground water coming in."

Word went to the top. To the TV truck. To the network. To the world. The news flashed like fireworks. *Carole Peterson and the trapped miners have been located, uninjured and safe. It will be a few more hours before they can be reached and extricated.*

The church bell rang. People gathered there, hugged each other, as did those waiting in the yard.

Restrained celebrations of hope stirred through the crowd.

Jess called into the pipe. "Great, Morrissey. We're working. Is Carole Peterson, okay?"

"Yeah. Everybody."

"Let me speak to her."

"Carole?"

"Hellooo?" called Carol.

"This is Jess Carter."

"What?"

"JESS CAR-TER."

"I knew it," said Carole to the others. "Can you get us out?" she called.

"You bet. What do you need?"

"Lots of water around us. We're hungry. Can you send us a cook?"

"A *book*?"

"A *cook*, as in <u>food</u>!"

Jess paused for a moment. Shook his head. *Yeah, right.* "I'll get back to you."

Jeez, can you believe her, Jess thought. A cook, yet. What spunk. Some woman. He reported the good news to the top.

"She wants a what?" someone asked in the news truck. Carole's tongue-in-cheek request for a cook went out on the airwaves.

In another hour, the crew had managed to insert a larger pipe in place of the original one, about four and a half inches in diameter. They flushed the mud out with a pressure hose.

"Hey, you guys," a distant male voice shouted, "what are you trying to do, drown us?"

"Couldn't fit a cook in the pipe," yelled Jess. "We're pushing through candy bars and drinking water. You're gonna need all your strength. Getting you out is gonna take a while."

Jess knew the temperature in the cave-in space could easily approach 100 degrees. They could dehydrate.

By the time the connecting flight of Carole's sister landed in Pittsburgh the news had been broadcast. The US Air pilot had relayed the latest word to the passengers and the story was on every TV monitor in the airport. After an hour layover she caught a prop flight to Haversford, ecstatic that her sister was alive and apparently unhurt. She went directly to the mine and checked in with authorities. Superintendent Lavery assured her the best guy in the business was heading operations and things looked hopeful.

Pastor McCrae gave thanks to 'the glory of God' that so many good people were spared. People flocked to the church again. More hymns of praise and thanksgiving rocked the building.

Mary Elizabeth Carter awoke in her bed and heard the news. She stood before her crucifix, gave thanks, then blew out the candle.

By now the Beltson Mine yard was packed with media trucks from as far away as Chicago. Scores of reporters were interviewing anyone who would speak with them about the hazards of coal mining, prodding for comments on fatal accidents at Beltson Mine. But few in the crowd were forthcoming. They were more interested in those still trapped. Microphone wires and cables crisscrossed the area like disorganized spaghetti. Floodlights filled the company yard.

Down below, Jess prepared to shove a tube-like package of small bottles of water and candy bars through the pipe. "Stuff's coming through," Jess yelled. "Get ready. It's coming now." Carefully the package was eased through the pipe, pushed by connected rods.

In a few minutes Jess heard a faintly discerned voice. "Thanks. Got it. Morrissey here. We got a problem. Water's coming in from somewhere. Ice cold. Maybe an underground stream ruptured or something. Can't tell yet. It's two feet deep and rising. We're cold."

"Mr. Morrissey, wait," said Carole, "don't send that rod back through the pipe to them yet." She handed a small video cartridge in a plastic bag to one of the miners. He wrapped tape around the bag and lashed it to the rod."

"Okay, pull out the rod now," Morrissey yelled again into the pipe. "Careful. There's something on the end of it."

A few minutes later Jess Carter called back, "What's this cassette tape for?"

"Miss Peterson wants it sent up to the TV truck. Jess, the water's rising faster. How much longer?"

"About two hours."

"We'll be under water by then."

"Morrissey, get everybody to the back of the shaft. There's a wide clearing about a hundred feet back just before the end. The shaft angles up there and the ground gets higher. "

"I hope it's high enough, Jess. Water is pouring in now."

"You've got to try it. Hang on. We'll get you out."

Jess sent word to the top that they were in steady contact with the 'trapped eight,' and that everyone, including Carole Peterson, was still okay. No injuries. They had adequate air, but the shaft was flooding. The trapped people were seeking higher ground farther into the shaft. Most likely an underground stream had fractured a wall during the cave-in. Jess and his crew accelerated their pace. They hoped to reach them in time.

Thirty minutes later, Morrissey called through the pipe, barely audible now, "Jess, Jess! It's up to my waist now and ice cold. I walked to the end of the shaft. There's water all the way. Not deep there. But it's filling up. I sent everyone back there. Gotta leave this place now. Hurry up you guys."

"Can't we drain the water out through the pipe?" a rescuer asked Jess.

"The shaft slopes down from here. It's much lower where they are," said Jess. "The water can't flow up to us. The pumping system was cut off in that shaft when it was closed down. Call up top. We need portable extraction pumps and hose *now*! And get the auger drill ready." *Hold on, Carole,* he said *sotto voce. We'll get you, I promise.*

Jess had dedicated his life to rescues. He had given his word. He would do it. But the stakes were getting higher and the odds shorter.

News of the rapidly deteriorating situation flashed across the media. Once again the outlook was grave. Company management quickly released a statement: *Beltson Mine company geologists confirm the existence of an underground stream in the vicinity of North Shaft Three. The shaft was abandoned some time ago. The stream has apparently broken through and water is seeping into the shaft. It is not known why the trapped party entered the shaft. Every effort is being made to reach them as quickly as possible.*

The new information upset everyone. It was nearly ten o'clock at night. Pastor McCrae's church filled again. Mary Elizabeth Carter faulted herself for putting out the candle hours too soon. Families prayed together. The town's mood dimmed from cautious joy to desperate hope.

Carole's sister, anxiously waiting in the mine yard, hurried to the broadcast truck and identified herself.

By then the video tape had been passed up to the truck and was broadcast as *A Special Bulletin: We have just received a tape, recorded earlier by Carole Peterson deep in Beltson Mine. We are showing it to you now, unedited, just handed to us*—even though the engineer played it first for Carole's sister and company representatives.

Across the nation the TV appearance of Carole Peterson stunned viewers. Trapped deep in the earth, so calm in such a desperate situation, her poignant plea to Jess Carter to save them was run with every newscast. Radio stations carried sound bites. No one anywhere, it seemed, could any longer be oblivious to the plight of "the TV newswoman trapped with seven others in Beltson Coal Mine and now in danger of drowning."

Governor Rendell was on site holding a press conference, personally assuring all that everything possible was being done to extricate the trapped people quickly and safely.

Mary Elizabeth Carter relit her candle. She stood before her crucifix, wrapped the Rosary around her fingers. "Please, God, let them come home safe."

A pizza truck arrived at the yard. People inhaled the aroma even before they heard the driver say to a cop, "We got hot pizza for Carole Peterson and the miners." Restaurants from as far away as Pittsburgh sent meals.

Carole, her cameraman, the five miners, and Fergis sloshed their way in darkness through the rising water back toward the end of the shaft. Just as Jess had said, the ground rose the farther in they went. But the ceiling got lower also, so that by the time they reached the end of the shaft they could no longer stand up straight. Icy water covered their feet and was rising fast. It was just a matter of time.

"I can't swim. I can't swim," burst out Fergis.

Morrissey laughed. "Where the hell would you go if you could?"

"But, but, I mean…"

"Yeah, we know what you mean. It you were a fish and could see in the dark you'd slither out."

The guys laughed with a bravado men sometimes toss out at each other when facing danger.

"I can swim, Mr. Fergis,"slightly-built miner Peter Haase offered with a touch of whimsy. "It's easy. I'll teach you sometime."

"Yeah," said Morrissey, "all you gotta do is hold your breath for an hour." More laughter all around. Then it was quiet.

"Jess Carter said he'd get us out," said Carole. "I don't know how he'll do it, but I know he will or he'll die trying."

"Don't say that. Don't say that. I don't want to die," moaned Fergis.

In the main tunnel the rescue team had managed to clear away much of the cave-in debris, but there was still about forty feet to go. Jess sensed the time was now. He decided to try a risky procedure. "Pull out the four-inch pipe. Bring up the auger rig."

Hand over hand, they extracted the pipe. As soon as they did, mud and soft debris oozed back into the vacated tube-like cavity. Quickly they inserted the six-foot long auger, attached the cables and prod extensions and powered it up. In a few moments it was tearing into the softness of the hole, spitting out mud. Then with a roar it began gouging like a mad dog against the harder surfaces, through rock, through coal and dirt and collapsed timbers, ever widening the hole, until at last it was big enough for a man to crawl in. Five more feet or so and they'd be through to the other side.

"Come on, guys, a few more minutes and we've got it." Jess said.

The eight trapped people in North Shaft Three had gone as far as they could go. They huddled together against the far end wall and prayed. The water continued to rise.

"Hold on. Hold on. We'll get you," Jess muttered to himself. Then he commanded, "Okay, guys, pull out the auger. I'm going in. Everybody, heave. Now, hand me the small oxygen tank and scuba mask, and the light." Jess took off his heavy gear.

"Man, it's too a tight space and it's still unstable," said Lavery, who had rejoined the team. "That drill weakened stuff all around the hole. It could collapse. We need more time to line it and make sure it's okay, Jess. We don't want to lose you."

"We're out of time, Lou."

"It's too wild an idea. You don't even know where they are."

"I've got a pretty good idea. Let's get moving. Here's the plan. Tie this rope around my ankle, guys. The hole is kind of mushy so I can't be sure you'll hear me. As soon as I get to the other side I'll tug it; you tug back to confirm, then I'll untie it and let it go. Pull it out. Work the auger drill back and forth through hole again while I'm gone. We've got to make the opening larger. But be careful. Gently does it. In *exactly* ten minutes, pull the rig out and send the rope back attached to the rod.

"I'm going to get those people to the hole, one by one, and tie the rope under their arm pits. I'll tug on the line. Then you pull them through, but be careful. We'll repeat the process till everyone is out. Any questions?"

Lou Lavery spoke. "Jess, do you know what the chances are of this working out? Too many things can go wrong. Think it over."

"I do and I have. It's our only shot. The water is boss now. They'll drown or freeze. We have no choice."

Jess climbed over debris and slithered into the hole, inching forward on his elbows. He twisted and scraped along the sides, pushing the light and small scuba gear in front of him. Mud and pieces of rock fell as he slithered through. Almost blindly he willed himself ahead, dismissing thoughts of what could happen. This was not the time for speculation. *I will do this,* he said to himself.

At the end of the tube he dropped heavily into the cold water. It shocked him and renewed his sense of urgency. He knew he'd have to move quickly. Prolonged time in water this cold would cause hypothermia and make him lose consciousness. He slipped on the scuba mask then tugged the rope. When he felt their return tug, he released it, then for a moment watched it being withdrawn, a sliver of life vanishing into darkness.

He slipped off his shoes and swam underwater toward the far end of the shaft until he could stand. As he came closer, the others could see his light and yelled, "Here! We're over here!"

He explained to them how he was going to get them out one at a time. "Just hold onto me. We'll share the air mask till we get to the escape hole. I'll tie a rope around you and they'll pull you from the other end as you crawl out."

"Oh God, how are we ever going to see in all that dark water?" Fergis said in a panic.

"You won't see much," Jess answered. "Just hold on. And keep going."

"Okay, okay, take me first," Fergis said. "I'm a company vice-president and I've got a wife who needs me."

"Yeah, get him out of here," Haase, said.

"He's too heavy," said Jess. "Won't fit yet. Here's the way it's going to be. They're making the passage larger all the time. I don't want anyone to get stuck in it. So thin ones go first. Come on, Carole, grab hold. I'll help you. We've got to move fast. Trust me."

"I do."

"I'll be back in a few minutes, guys. Everybody wait here," Jess said.

"Like we had someplace to go," shrugged Haase, rolling his eyes.

Carole and Jess waded forward, Jess pointing the light, until Carole was chin deep in water. "Okay, Carole. Here we go. Hang on tight to me."

They submerged and took turns with the scuba mask until they reached the escape hole. The rope and rod were waiting. Jess tied the rope around Carole, tugged the line, yelled into the hole, "Okay" hoping they'd hear him, and told her to crawl through.

She kept hugging him. "Jess, Jess, be careful." She looked weak and cold.

"Don't quit, no matter what," he said, as she disappeared into the escape passage.

He swam back toward the others—the wait must seem like forever to them, he knew.

Underwater he welcomed the vibrating sound of the auger drill attacking again, distant as a dream. It meant Carole had made it through.

"You're next, skinny cameraman," said Jess when he reached them. "Ditch the camera." When the two of them made it to the hole, Jess quickly tied the rope around him and gave it a stiff yank. Feeling the return tug, he said, "Okay, go for it, buddy. Just keep moving."

He made four more trips through the numbing water and took four more men out safely. By now fatigue and exposure had weighted his arms and legs. He labored to swim. His body was sluggish. Each breath he took was an extreme effort. The shock of cold knifed the length of his backbone. He knew what was coming.

At the entrance of the escape passage the water was already only inches from the ceiling. He was alert enough to know he would run out of time. Only one more trip could be made and there were still two people to rescue, Morrissey and Fergis. Whichever one was left would surely drown.

He plunged in again. As soon as he could stand near the far end, he tightened his stomach muscles as hard as he could. He did the same with all the muscle groups in his body. Then he released them. He knew repeated muscle contractions could produce some body heat and force more circulation. He continued the process then waded up the high ground.

By this time, Carole and some of the others had been taken safely to the surface. Ambulances were parked nearby, motors running. Two medivac choppers waited, should they be needed to rush survivors to the Hyperbaric Chamber at Allegheny General Hospital in Pittsburgh.

As Carole was carried out of the mine on a stretcher attended by paramedics, she raised a hand weakly to the crowd. Huge cheers went up. "Carole, Carole, how was it down there?" an excited TV reporter asked, reaching past attendants and stretching a microphone to her face.

"If it weren't for Jess Carter, she said, barely audible, "we'd all be dead." With that, she was loaded into an ambulance and driven away, accompanied by her sister.

Television carried the scene live. *Carole Peterson has just been brought up from the mine. She appears to be weak but fully conscious and is being taken to Haversford Hospital. Other survivors are being brought up as we speak."*

Each of the miners briefly told of their incredible escape from the flooded shaft and expressed awe and gratitude for Jess Carter.

Mary Elizabeth searched for her son in the scenes beings shown on TV. No sign of him.

The Governor noted the extraordinary efforts of the brave rescue crew.

Pastor McCrae and the congregation were not in the church. They were waiting near the mine entrance with the rest of the crowd.

At the far end of the shaft Jess spoke to the two remaining men. "I can't make two more trips before this water fills to the ceiling."

Morrissey spoke up. "Listen, Jess. I got a plan. I was a *champeen* swimmer in high school. It's only a hundred feet or so. I can make it underwater half way without air. You and Fergis can share the air tank. I'll be along side of you. I'll tug you when I'm out of air. Then give me a hit from the air mask and I'll make it the rest of the way. Whaddaya say?"

"You're not a kid anymore, Morrissey," said Jess. "Think you can do it?"

"No, no, no. Take me first," pleaded Fergis.

"Hmm. You're on, Morrissey, let's go for it. Fergis, you hold on to me. We're going in … the three of us together, just like Morrissey said." They waded into the numbing water, then submerged.

Fergis kept grabbing in the darkness for Jess's air mask. Jess struggled to control him. Morrissey labored to stay with them, taking air twice. They made it.

Red-faced, Morrissey gasped as they finally surfaced at the hole. "See, I told you."

Fergis sputtered and coughed. "Oh, my God. Oh, my God."

"Now listen, Fergis," Jess said, as he tied the rope around him, "when you get through tell them no more auger drill. The hole's big enough. Be sure and tell them. Just send the rope and rod back. We're ready now. Don't forget."

"Yes, yes," said Fergis, shivering like a frozen ghost, He crawled into the hole.

Jess waited several minutes for the return of the rope. He yelled into the passage. No one answered. No rope. No rod. Nothing. "Damn Fergis," he muttered.

"Hey, Jess," Morrissey said weakly, his teeth chattering, as the two men treaded water, their faces pressed to the ceiling, "the TV gal, Carole, said she knew you would get us out. She a friend of yours?" Morrissey struggled to stay afloat.

"Never met her before." Jess remembered holding her close as they swam underwater to the escape passage. She was smaller than she looked on TV. It seemed days ago.

This had been a day much more challenging than he thought it would be, though he had to admit luck had been with them so far. It was homestretch time. He grabbed two long deep breaths and gathered his strength for the final effort. He had to get Morrissey out now.

"You okay, buddy?" he asked Morrissey.

"Everything hurts, Jess." His voice was weak and gravelly.

They were both exhausted. Jess knew time was critical. They waited for the rope. It didn't come. "Damn Fergis," Jess muttered. "We've got to crawl out on our own … now. We can't wait for the rope, Morrissey.

Come on, I'll lead the way. Hold onto me. Think you can make it?"

"Maybe," Morrissey puffed. "I can't last much longer."

Just then the rod and rope appeared. "It's here, Morrissey! Come on." Jess climbed into the passage, tugged the rope. "Hang on to me, buddy. Let's go. We can do this." He was so cold he could hardly feel the rope as he gripped it with one hand and started to push forward on his stomach, holding the light in front of him. Morrissey grabbed Jess's ankle and held tightly; suddenly, he let go. Jess stopped. The rod and rope kept going.

He heard Morrissey splash back and bubble under. Jess let go of the light and inched backward pushing himself with his elbows until he fell into the water. By the time he found Morrissey in the darkness, grabbed him and got his face clear of the water, Morrissey was limp.

"Come on, man, breathe," Jess said, as he tried to administer mouth-to-mouth while treading water. "NO," said Jess. "NO. Come on, man! Hang on! We're going to make it. We're almost there."

Morrissey slumped heavily in Jess's arms; he never revived. Jess held him up as long as he could, then had to let him slip away. He grabbed onto the wall, trying to keep his head above water.

"NO," Jess yelled again—but this time not to Morrissey. He felt an ominous rumble shake the walls of the shaft as a flood of mud came tumbling out of the escape passage. Muck regurgitated from the hole then stopped. But the rumbling continued. Jess knew what was coming. He considered his options; there was only one. He threw himself up into the escape hole and began crawling furiously through the muck.

On his stomach, arms in front of him, he pawed and clawed in pitch blackness, inching forward. For a while it worked, and Jess was hopeful. But the mud, mixing with loosening dirt, got thicker, and the more he tried to push it aside, the more it gathered around him — there was nowhere else for it to go—until at last, as if squashed under the foot of an elephant, he could no longer make headway. He tried to wriggle forward, but his strength was spent. He was imprisoned and powerless in the packed mud. There was little air, perhaps a minute or two left.

How does a man feel when he knows death is imminent? Does he curse his luck? Does he plead and pray for a miracle? Does he make peace with his God? Or does he despair and weep, declaring his love for ones he would leave behind?

As he lay there, Jess was aware his final moments had come. His first reaction was that it seemed impossible; there must be a way. But logic told him there was none. Ironically, he had managed to crawl into his own sealed coffin. He was too exhausted and numb with cold to fight any longer. He waited calmly for the end, perhaps like countless others before him in the mines, saying goodbye, resigning himself peacefully to the inevitable. He thought of his mother and his early promise to her.

He closed his eyes and saw his father smiling at him, leaving the house years ago to go to work. "Hi, Dad," Jess said, as he reached out, man to man, to grasp his hand.

Thirty miles away in Aliquippa, Mary Elizabeth Carter awoke in her bedroom chair and sat upright. The candle flame wobbled, flickered, then went out. She bowed her head, closed her eyes and wept silently.

A minute or so later the entire ceiling of North Shaft Three let go with a roar. Thousands of tons of pressured rock and coal thundered down, packing solid the water-filled cavern.

In seconds tons of displaced water exploded up into the narrow escape passage, surging ahead with the power of a raging flood. It bulldozed into Jess, pushing his prone body ahead, scooping mud and everything else in its path, until all spewed out into the main tunnel near the terrified rescue crew.

Jess lay there unconscious. They began working on him with oxygen and CPR, but with little hope.

In a few moments Jess heard a voice say, "Now how the hell did he do that?"

**

Caught...
*In Florida*_____

"If you know a better way," Henry said, tired of defending himself, "why don't you drive?"

"Tsk." His wife rolled her eyes.

He flipped on the overhead light, spread out a map, laid it on the dash, partially blocking his view of the road.

"My God," his wife said, "what are you doing now? I thought you knew the way?"

He slowed the car to a stop and studied the map. "Yeah, this road will work," he said aloud, reassuring himself, not really responding to her. He flicked off the overhead and got under way again. He began to sing. "Somewhere over the rainbow, blue birds fly, my wife knows the directions ... oh why the hell don't I."

"Very funny."

"Come on, loosen up."

Henry was used to having his own way when he drove, and he didn't appreciate his wife constantly questioning his judgment lately. She'd keep chipping away at him, like he had half a brain. "You sure we've got enough gas?" "Watch out for that car." "Did you lock-up the house when we left?" "Don't forget to take in the mail tomorrow."

Now that he was no longer employed, for the first time in his life, he came to see marriage from a new perspective. It seemed to him that as soon as guys retire, wives start taking over. Like they should be in charge of everything. Like they've been patiently putting up with the guy's bumbling all these years, but now, since he's no longer working, they're completely justified in taking over his life. Okay, so sometimes a man's socks don't match. But hey, so what? That doesn't mean he's *non compos mentis.*

He never questioned the way she did things around the house that he would have done differently. No. They were her choices. He stayed out of it. Henry figured some things are the natural domain of women... like whether your socks match or not. But driving a car...that's always a guy thing. So why did she always have to make a scene when he was behind the wheel?

"Why didn't you park over there?" or "you're driving too close to the car ahead," or "do you have to pass everybody on the road?" Which of course he didn't, only the slow pokes, mostly women who drove like they were browsing for nothing in particular at the mall. Man, they're dangerous.

Today Henry could tell by the way the short trip was starting out it would be another forum for his wife to assert her infinite wisdom in matters that were in the domain of maledom. He could feel another un-meeting-of-the–minds coming. This time he resolved to keep his cool and not let her get to him, no matter what. He knew it took two to make an argument. He decided singing might get her in a better mood. Of course that didn't work.

"It doesn't seem right to me," she said. "We didn't come this way the last time we went to their house."

"This is a short cut, sweetie," he said, with a half smile, "a new road. It says so on the map."

"Oh boy, a map. How clever. Why didn't we come the way we did before?"

"I know what I'm doing."

"Ah, Henry the Great, been everywhere, knows everything, remembers nothing."

"Okay, okay, sometimes I forget things."

"Well, shouldn't we have been there by now then? It's getting dark and there's no sign of life on this road."

"Oh, don't worry. I've got it covered. Don't you ever get tired of taking the same routes all the time? Come on, where's your sense of adventure?" He wasn't being argumentative. This line of reasoning made perfect sense to Henry. Life could get boring at his age. Varying the travel routes was one way of adding a little variety, a little zest, sometimes even a challenge.

She refused to go along with his attempts to soften her mood. Apparently, she felt this was not the time for levity. He could sense what was coming.

"Well, I like to go a way I can depend on, one that I'm sure of. You can experiment all you want when you're alone. But please, not with me in the car. Not when we have to get somewhere on time. I hate being late. It isn't right."

"We're not late."

"Not yet," she said, "but we will be in another ten minutes."

Twilight surrendered to darkness. The road was quiet. A procession of clouds kept the moon at bay, preventing it from assuming its role as the featured luminary of the nightscape.

Ten more minutes.

"Ah, I think I should have taken a left on that road back about a mile or so. I'm going to turn around and try it."

"I told you this wasn't a good idea. We're lost. Admit it."

"We're not lost."

"Well, where are we then?"

"I don't know exactly."

"Then we're lost."

"I know where I'm going."

"You're going to be late. That's where you're going. You and your short cuts. It happens all the time. Why are you stopping the car now?"

"Too noisy in here. Can't concentrate. I'm going to get out and collect my thoughts … ahem, while I make a little nature call."

"Out here? Now? My Gawd."

"Don't you ever get tired of finding fault?"

She seemed to be ready for his remark and unleashed an assault that likely had been simmering just below her epidermis. "We're miles from who-knows-where. It's pitch black. We're on some back road you think *may* be a short cut. We're late. We're lost. Now you're stopping to relieve yourself like some animal. And you have the nerve to accuse me of finding fault? That's disgusting."

"Okay, I won't get out then. I'll pee in the car."

"Don't be smart. You know what I mean. Besides, you should have taken care of that before we left the house."

"I would have, but I ran out of time."

"You had plenty of time to get ready."

"I'm just saying, when you scowled at me and made that face when we were walking out the door and said, '*You're going like that?*' I thought I'd better change."

"Well, you looked terrible."

"Audrey, we're not in Michigan now. This is Florida."

"I know that."

"It's casual. I don't care if I ever see a suit and tie again."

"I'm not talking about a suit and tie. I bought you some nice dressy sport shirts. Why don't you wear one of those once in a while? They certainly look better than those tee shirts and khaki shorts you live in."

"Okay, okay. You're right. That's just why I went back and changed my clothes, so I'd look the way you want me too. Just took a little time."

"Well, it's not my fault we're late. And it's not my fault we're on this god-forsaken road either."

"I didn't say it was."

"That's what you meant."

"Look, I'll be right back. I got to go water the bushes." He left the motor running, the headlights on, got out, leaving a fuming Audrey. He made his way to the back of the car.

Recently he had overheard her remark to her friend that the older he got "the more he doesn't seem to care about his appearance and the more chances he seems to take driving. Why doesn't he pay more attention? It's a wonder he doesn't have an accident."

The marsh-like savannas on both sides of the road, forbidden territory at night, harbored many of Florida's indigenous creatures, from beastie bugs and mosquitoes to wild pigs, poisonous snakes, Florida panthers and ubiquitous alligators.

The road cut right across "their" homesteaded territory like an ugly asphalt intrusion. The two-lane blacktop strip was elevated on land-fill a few feet above the ground level of the savannas. A six-foot-wide grassy shoulder, trimmed of most large vegetation, separated each side of the road from the semi-dry marsh. Beyond this margin of clearing, low brush quickly thickened, swampy in summer, parched in winter. Judging by the speed with which most motorists drove across this stretch, people seemed to have no interest in meeting the nocturnal creatures that lurked there.

The moon made its appearance just as Henry found a nice spot by a tree just beyond the shoulder about fifteen feet to the rear of the car. He proceeded to do what he set out to do, feeling the intense sudden relief of the real 'pause that refreshes'.

He looked up at the stars. There seemed to be billions of them tonight. How quiet. How peaceful. How awesome. The air steamed on the ground in front of him from the newly deposited moisture. Ah, he was in no hurry to return to the car. It was serene here. Too bad his wife felt he was such a screw-up. *She takes everything so seriously. God knows, you have to have a sense of humor to survive in this world. Laugh and the world laughs with you, that's what I say.*

At this moment he felt as if he were part of the heavens. He imagined he could reach up, touch them, and, hand-over-hand, from star to star, traverse the universe.

Audrey turned on the car radio and fiddled with the tuning until she found a local FM station, one that played mostly classical music. But there was no music at the moment. Instead an announcer was saying, "*... and that's when the two convicted murder-rapists made their escape from the Fort Pierce courthouse. Police have advised area residents to remain in their homes and lock their doors.*"

Immediately, Audrey leaned over and locked both doors of the eight-year-old Chrysler. "*The Sheriff's department has set up roadblocks on all key county roads. Until the escapees, whom authorities have described as armed and extremely dangerous, are caught, residents should exercise caution and stay inside. Reportedly, one guard was stabbed during the escape and died. Once again, two dangerous criminals have ... *"

Henry completed his long and willing effort to assist nature, watching the starlit heavens until clouds floated in again and blocked his view. He gave his zipper a quick upward tug. But there was something important he forgot to do.

"Owoo," he cried. "Damn! Ow. Shit." Suddenly the shimmering heavens lost their glow.

The stars he saw now were in his head. A vital part of him was inextricably snared in the clutches of the zipper monster.

He tried pulling and tugging and pushing, but it only made matters worse. He was stuck. I've got to get help, he thought. "Audrey. Hey, Audrey." No response.

With one hand pressing down between his pant legs to prevent the zipper from furthering its death grip, he waddled on tiptoes slowly and painfully up onto the road, hunched over, wiggling carefully to the passenger side of the car.

All was dark and quiet except for Beethoven booming from the car radio. Desperately he pounded on the window with his free hand. His wife screamed in fright and ducked. She stretched out across the seat, reached for the horn and held her hand on it, blasting it into the echoing night.

Henry yelled, "Audrey, open up. It's me. Open up!" But she couldn't hear him. He pounded on the window again. The horn kept blaring. He pressed his face against the window. "Audrey. Audrey. It's me."

He gimped his way to the front of the car and stood facing her in the beam of head-lights. He pounded on the hood. She peeked through the steering wheel, still not releasing the horn. She saw it was her husband. He appeared to be in pain, looking disheveled and distraught.

She let go of the horn, got out of the car and ran to him. "Oh, honey, what happened?" As she spoke, she looked down and saw what the problem was. "What on earth were you doing?"

He grimaced and said, "I was fishing. I couldn't reel in the pole. What the hell do you think I was doing?"

Seeing him standing there fully exposed in the harsh glare of the headlights, with his pants drooping toward his knees, Audrey broke into a fit of laughter. She doubled over, slapped the car-hood, threw her head back. "Oh, Henry, that's the best one ever."

"Damn it, Audrey, this is serious. Fine time to be laughing. I'm in pain. I need help NOW."

She moved closer, getting a better view. "Aha," she said, "you got yourself good this time, didn't you?"

"It's not my fault. Something's wrong with the zipper. I haven't worn these pants since they came back from the cleaners. I shouldn't have changed clothes."

"Let me take a look." She put one hand on him and the other on the zipper and with a steady pull tried to liberate him.

"Ow!"

"Sorry." She bent down. Looked closer. "Let me see." She saw that Henry was definitely pinched. She fiddled with the zipper. Tried to ease it back slowly. It wouldn't budge. She tried pulling at the cloth material, kneading it back and forth, trying to separate the fabric from the teeth of the zipper. That didn't work.

"Maybe the doctor will have to amputate," she offered.

"Audrey, this is serious. Get me out of this!" Henry looked down at her working on him then up to the stars again. That's when he saw the car approaching. It pulled alongside. An intruding spotlight flashed upon them.

After a moment, from the passenger side an officer called over to them. "Sorry, folks, this isn't a lovers lane. You'll have to find someplace else to do that."

"What?!" said Henry.

"It's not safe on this road tonight, folks. You'd better move along."

Audrey stood up from her kneeling position and walked over to the police car, smiling, looking trim and elegant.

"Officers, my husband is having a little problem. I wonder if you'd mind helping him."

"You serious, lady?"

She chuckled slightly and said in a sweet tone, "My husband went to the *bathroom* over there and caught himself in his zipper."

"Oh, hmm. Well, let's see." The two officers got out of the patrol car, came over to Henry and carefully evaluated his predicament Finally, with the aid of pliers, WD-40 and latex gloves they managed to free Henry from the tenacious grip of the zipper. As his wife muffled giggles, Henry, grateful to be free, made a feeble effort to grumble a gruff, "Thanks, guys."

"Oh, you bet, sir. These things can be dangerous, that's for sure," one said as they got back into the patrol car. Henry could see them burst into laughter when they were inside.

"You drive," Henry deferred to his wife. Once behind the wheel Audrey lowered her window, waved and called, "Thank you, officers. We're trying to find Glades View Road."

"Oh sure, just follow us, Ma'am," one said. We'll wait till you get going."

Both cars drove slowly away in a quiet caravan.

Henry sat in silence, grumpy at first. Then he remembered the wind-swept, snow-covered Michigan countryside at this time of year. Things could be worse.

A warm breeze from the south brushed the savannas. Near the road, close to where the cars had been, a clump of bushes stirred almost imperceptively. Perhaps the wind. Or had a stealthy animal of the marsh decided to patrol its territory in the darkness or maybe cross the road?

Dark clouds passed from time to time, permitting intermittent patches of moonlight that bathed the terrain temporarily, as if glowing a deserted prison yard. In one such illuminated moment the Man in the Moon, had he been watching, might have caught a glimpse of two sinister creatures lurking along side the road, crouched behind scrub palmettos, apparently readying to pounce on unprotected prey.

**

The Flag...
A Vermont Story_____

The Vermont winter had not been easy on Darryl's American Flag. It had never been left out all winter before, and now it was tattered to a washed-out version of itself. The lines were so twisted Darryl couldn't lower it. He made a few attempts to untangle them, overlapping them, snapping them vigorously, but that didn't work. He couldn't move the flag up or down. As winter set in, the lines began to freeze, so he gave up.

Darryl's flag hung atop a ten-foot wooden pole he had inserted vertically into a polyurethane sleeve in the concrete front porch of his house. He considered gripping the pole at its base and yanking it out of the sleeve. But he knew it was wedged in tightly with ice and snow. He didn't think his blood pressure could stand the sudden strain it would take to unseat it. So he didn't even try to lift it out. He just sulked that this was another one of the crummy things about getting old.

Everything gets rusty or wears out … hips, knees, feet, heart, muscles, back. Then prostate problems. Blood pressure goes screwy. Cholesterol gets out of whack. Even breathing takes effort. It's always something. It's the pits.

He was too proud or too stubborn, or both, to ask anyone who came to visit him, not that that many people did these days, to help him retrieve the flag.

He'd wait till spring when the weather was better and the snow was mostly gone. Maybe he'd ask his son to help when he came up from Virginia this year for a visit. *Yep, good idea.* He agreed with himself to wait for his son.

A pair of sturdy black andirons squatted in the living room's oversized fieldstone fireplace, ready to support another hearty wood fire. A large black metal screen guarded the fieldstone hearth from spewing crackles of flying embers. A few multi-colored braided rugs were scattered about on the pegged, wide boards of the hard wood floor. Except for a leather lounge chair, the furniture was mostly maple.

White-haired, heavier than he should be, puffy eyed from not sleeping well, Darryl usually ensconced himself in his favorite chair near the front bay windows. Whenever he looked around the room he felt comfortable with the way it was, the way it had always been, solid, warm, dependable.

Before the start of the snowy winter his American flag had waved proudly in front of the house, like a beacon of solid Vermont, letting the world know that the large house on a hill just off Route 67 stood for good old American values—free enterprise, hot dogs, baseball, the Sunday afternoon NFL games, corn on the cob, Notre

Dame football, hunting, fishing, and of course more cable television.

But the tri-colored symbol of the nation's greatness looked forlorn and defeated now, just the way Darryl felt. He sat there day after day, tired and disheveled, his once-proud crown of wavy white-fox hair uncombed, his matted beard untrimmed.

He had fought in the South Pacific in World War II. He remembered battles at Tarawa and the Solomon's and what the Stars and Stripes had meant to him and to his buddies—it kept them going. More than half his men lay buried in those faraway places. He was one of the lucky ones and he never forgot it. The flag was sacred to him. It pained him now to see it like that, a prisoner of nature. To make matters worse, during a recent storm the winter winds had twisted the flag in such a way that it was now hanging upside down. But even so, his arthritic aches and pains convinced him not to try to retrieve it.

One frigid February day a neighbor from a nearby farm came by in his pickup. He trudged about 150 feet up the small hill on the snow-covered driveway to Darryl's two-story clapboard house. It was a gray house with a bright blue front door and more windows than it seemed to need. The neighbor rang the bell.

"Is something wrong, Darryl?"

"Why should anything be wrong?" he snapped. "I'm just fine. What's wrong with you?"

"Well, Darryl," the neighbor said, "your flag's been lookin' like shit lately. And now it's flyin' upside-down. Means distress in my book."

"Yeah, yeah, I see. Didn't notice. I'll take care of it. 'Preciate it, Roy. Thanks."

But as the flag remained marooned in its sorry state, Darryl sank deeper into depression. In March a woman from the town's Daughters of the American Revolution, the D.A.R., watch dogs of proper respect to the Flag, telephoned offering to replace the flag.

"Don't bother me," he grumped. "I'll take care of it." He hung up. But the truth was, ever since the flag had been flying upside-down, something else besides his failing health and the weather compelled him to leave it there. Seeing the flag in its present sorry state had stirred latent feelings of guilt, feelings that had almost consumed him for a time after his wife's accident. Now they had returned and haunted him incessantly. He didn't feel he deserved to have the flag hanging properly. This was his punishment for everyone to see.

His daughter called from California. His grandson would soon graduate from college with honors. And did he "want to come out for the ceremony and visit?"

"Honors, eh? Must take after me. Hah. Nope. No trips like that for me anymore."

"How *are* you feeling, Dad?"

"Me? Fine, fine."

"Anything you need? Is the cleaning woman coming in every week?"

"Uh huh."

"Louise still cooking your dinners? She picking up the mail for you?"

"Yep, right. Don't need nothin'. Doin' fine."

"Dad, I worry about you. It's been over a year since we lost Mom. I'm worried about you living alone. Why don't you sell the place and come out here and live with us?"

"Why the hell would I want to do that? Wouldn't know what to do in California. Too many weirdoes out there. Like it here just fine. I'm okay. Thanks all the same."

"But supposing something should happen to you?"

"Nothin's gonna happen to me. Besides, I got Scooch with me."

"A dog can't use the telephone if you get sick or fall or something."

"Never even get a cold. Feeling fine. Gotta go now. Bye." He hung up.

Had it really been that long? Had a year passed already since Edna's accident? He missed her. He could still hear her that fatal day telling him to sit up straight as he relaxed in his favorite chair.

"Slouching's bad for your back, Darryl. You know that."

"Now why would I be sitting in a comfortable chair if I wanted to sit up straight? I'm comfortable here. That's what this chair's fo-wah. Why don't you stop naggin' and just go tend to the laundry or something. Seems to me you been puttin' it off."

"Darryl, you're getting to be a stubborn old coot."

"Yeah, yeah." He went back to watching a football game. The busy fire in the fireplace crackled like beavers snapping twigs. He liked the sound.

He heard the kitchen door creak open, the click of the light switch, her first heavy step, and then almost immediately a terrible rumble as she tumbled over and over down the stairs onto the concrete cellar floor. Then all was quiet. "Edna!" he called. "Edna?" He waited. Nothing. He hurried into the kitchen. From the top of the stairs he saw her at the bottom lying in a heap, motionless. He called 911.

His wife, his life-long companion, died before the paramedics got her to the hospital. Skull fracture and heart failure.

In the weeks following the funeral Darryl realized he had left his hammer on the top step after he had fixed a sticky dresser drawer. *Don't feel like bringing it all the way down to the workbench just now. I'll do it later.* He had forgotten to put it away. He had been forgetting things more and more these days. She must have stepped on it, lost her footing and fell. He knew it, even though he didn't see the hammer when he saw her down there on the floor. *It must have fallen into the cellar.* He never did care to go down there anymore.

For fifty-two years Edna and Darryl had been married, always taking care of each other. He couldn't forgive himself after she fell. He had to live with the fact that he was responsible for her death. He never mentioned the hammer to anyone. No one ever asked. But the secret wore heavily on him until it gradually faded into his closet of clouded memories. That is, until now. If Edna were around she'd be buggin' me about the flag, he thought.

"You should know better, letting that flag hang out there like that," she would say.

She was right about most things, not that he let her think so, and she'd have been right about the flag, that's for sure. Now every time he looked out the window at the flag hanging upside down, he thought about her crashing down the cellar stairs, and the hammer.

One day he could have sworn she was outside looking in at him. "Come on Darryl, get the lead out. Get on with it. What are you sitting around for?"

He blinked, looked again. She was gone. It was as if the distressed flag, stuck like that, was telling him it was his fault, reminding him that Edna would be around today if it hadn't been for the hammer.

Spring came in full that year, a bit chilly, but not unusual for Vermont. Irises pushed folded tips up into the light of the world. Patches of snow and ice held out, refusing to yield until forced to shrink and surrender to inevitable meltdowns. Sparrows started greeting sunrises, pecking at the ground for the day's first meal. And on the porch the upside-down flag still hung limp, like a flimsy grave-marker for Edna.

His son Mark drove up from Virginia, as he did every April, arriving late one night. He parked his car around back and came in the kitchen door. Darryl looked forward to seeing him. He had showered and spruced up a bit. He was proud of his son and enjoyed his company every year. This time, however, after the usual small talk, Darryl didn't feel like getting into conversation the way he usually did. He was preoccupied with his own thoughts. He couldn't even manage to muster up enthusiasm for the fancy new fishing hat his son had brought for him.

"What's the matter, Pop? You feeling sick?"

"Ah, little of this, a little of that. You know how it is. Guess I'm just tired. Some days I get like this. Nothing to worry about. I think I'll go to bed. It's late. You take the upstairs guest room, like always, Mark. Stay up as late as you like. TV's working fine up there, I 'bleve. I'll see you in the morning."

That night Darryl dreamed he died in the South Pacific. He was on a barren hilltop and a bayoneted rifle marked his grave, stuck in the ground with a small upside-down flag hanging from it. A voice said, "You look like shit, Darryl, and so does your flag." Another said, "We'll get him a new one." Then the bayonet morphed into a hammer and tumbled faster and faster down the hill toward a bulldozer that was clearing brush for an airstrip. It clanged off a boulder, ricocheted up, hit the driver in the head and killed him. "I didn't mean to," Darryl cried out from his grave. "I forgot it." He woke up exhausted.

The next morning, he was already sitting at the solid-maple kitchen table having his coffee, black, no sugar, when his son came downstairs, obviously rested and ready to set about the usual spring fix-ups for his father.

"Great day, Pop. Slept like a log. Looks beautiful outside."

"Uh-huh, I guess."

"What do you have for me to do this trip? Roof repairs? Fix garage doors? Take down the storm windows? Patch screens. You name it."

"A few chores, the usual. Well, one thing in particular I'd thought we'd do first. But I guess it can wait till after we have some bacon and eggs. Got it cookin' already."

"Works for me. And if you've got more of that coffee, I'll have a cup. By the way, Pop, I found this hammer on the floor under the dresser in the bedroom this morning when I was putting on my shoes. You must be missing one." With that, he held the hammer out to his father then set it on the table. Darryl was speechless.

He stared at it. His eyes opened wide. His jaw dropped. In that moment he realized he hadn't left the hammer on the cellar stairs. All the while it had been where he last used it to fix the upstairs bedroom dresser.

"You OK, Pop?" his son said.

Darryl took a quick breath, sat up tall and said, "Mark, you 'spose you could help me take down the flag out on the front porch, now, before we eat?"

"Sure, Pop, no problem. Let's get to it. I'm hungry."

They walked through the living room, out the front door onto the cement porch. Darryl led the way. "Help me lift the pole from the holder," he said. "It's stuck real bad. I'll grab it low; you grab it high. We'll yank it out."

But as soon as Darryl gave it a little tug, it came flying up in his hands before his son even touched it. He laid it over a porch railing and his son easily untangled the flag and unclipped it from the imprisoning ropes.

Together they stretched it out and folded it neatly into a triangular configuration.

"Thought you said it was stuck, Pop."

"Thought it was," Darryl said.

**

Tattoo...
Forever Or Not_____

Brad sipped a hazelnut coffee from his *Go Gators* mug. A perfect way to laze through the Sunday morning newspaper, slouched in comfort, long legs stretched out under a table at his favorite campus java joint, unshaven, relaxed. His usual weekend ritual.

Looking chic and confident in her pale green warm-up suit, a co-ed made her way through the chatty crowd, found his table, and stood behind him as he looked at the newspaper.

The Gainesville Sun's big-type headline seemed to celebrate its proclamation:

KILLER PROF GETS DEATH PENALTY

Everyone knew the story. After a campus co-ed broke off their stormy relationship, she was murdered and partly dismembered by her lover. Not really a new story in today's world. But the killer in this case was a fully tenured, married chemistry professor, twenty-three years her senior. How could the bastard do it? Brad wondered. What gave him the right to take her life? No doubt he was obsessed with her—he must have been, but he should have been able to control his emotions. That's the true mark of an educated man—self-control. Good, the bastard's finally getting what he deserves.

"I can't say I agree with that decision," the woman's voice said clearly, as she peered over Brad's shoulder at the newspaper.

"What decision?" he said, not looking around to see who had spoken.

"Capital punishment, of course."

"Huh?" He swung around to confront the voice, ready to launch into an argument about the value of capital punishment both as a deterrent and as fitting retribution for heinous crimes. But facing him, a stunning young woman sipped her coffee matter-of-factly, as if strolling in an English garden, pausing to flick a speck of dust from her garment.

A rush of adrenaline invaded his solar plexus. In a corny movie the sound track would have gilded the moment with a choir of heavenly voices just as her velvet brown eyes melted into his brain. Always a sucker for brown eyes.

He tried to absorb the rest of her with a casual glance. Lustrous dark hair, pulled neatly to a pony tail. Alert face, gorgeous pink cheeks, peach skin. Provocative lips. A softly-defined athletic figure.

His mind clicked like a calculator. Nothing vague about her. She is totally in the moment and appears to know it.

She watched him make his assessment and smiled, not drawing her eyes away. Her warm-up jacket, unzipped at the top to the point of tasteful distraction, forced his eyes to dart momentarily toward what he guessed must be perfect breasts. She had a small but not fragile waist, which tapered out to trim, confident hips.

Moments like this did not occur often in Brad's life. In fact, when he thought about it, this was the only time it happened to him. It had been his habit to over-think encounters with attractive co-eds. He had dated several, never letting the immediate appeal of physical attributes override the un-appeal of what might later prove to be a dim intellect, in which case he would break off future dating with them.

He didn't consider this snobbery, but rather, he had standards, which came with the obligation of being a discerning person. Yet there he was, letting himself get worked up by a woman he'd just met. She had already managed to head off any thought of dim-wittedness. Obviously, she was bright, articulate and confident. He liked that.

Continuing where she left off, she said, "Capital punishment is barbaric, a throwback to the Hammurabi Code thousands of years ago—an eye for an eye, a tooth for a tooth. Remember? You're supposed to be a smart guy … the editor of the student newspaper, aren't you? You should know these things. Not a very civilized custom in today's day and age, not in *our* society. Besides, that prof might have had reasons we don't even know about."

Hmm, he thought, a brain that matches looks. He ahem-ed, sucked in a long breath and prepared to launch into his favorite pro-death-penalty speech. He had written a series of editorials on the subject. Of course he felt his views were well supported by facts.

But as he groped for a meaningful way to begin, he felt mesmerized by this interesting woman now challenging him to a duel. All he could muster was, "You've got a point there. Uh huh. Uh hum. Right, of course (*so much for clever repartee*). My name is Brad Engels."

"Yes, Bradley, I know who you are."

"You do?"

"I've read your editorials on capital punishment and I must say, I disagree completely. That's why I came over when I saw you. I'm Jennifer Raleigh." She extended her hand directly to him. He hurried to clasp it.

Brown eyes met blue eyes in wide-eyed consideration of possibilities. He took her expression as an invitation to date, or maybe debate. He wanted to impress her, say something clever, somehow get to know her. Instead he blundered out with, "This must be a dream. If it is, please don't wake me, because I can't believe what I'm seeing. You are so, so … wow!"

He knew he should have known better, blabbing drivel like a smitten sophomoric Cro-Magnon, as if blatant adoration was the way to score. Well duh, once the words are out, they're out. The damage had been done.

She could just as well have laughed. He thought she would; he looked pathetic and embarrassed enough. Instead, she glared at him with a look of righteous indignation coupled with exasperation. "Oh, forget it," she said, turned and sauntered away.

He sprang to his feet, took a couple of long strides, reached out an arm and tapped her on the shoulder. She flinched at his touch, as though her personal radar-protected zone had been violated. "Please excuse me,

Jennifer Raleigh, I apologize. That was so dumb. Please have coffee with me. I really want to hear what you have to say. Honestly, something got in the way of my brain."

"Oh? Is that what happened? I would have thought you had more substance."

"Mea culpa, mea maxima culpa," he said, tapping his fist lightly against his heart repeatedly, feigning a plea, bowing his head. "My fault," he added. "Really, I do want to talk with you." She smiled. He had broken through.

Talk they did. In the process he learned that Jennifer was in her second year of law school and was passionate about embarking on a law career. From the way she handled herself, Brad figured she would excel at the law, and it wouldn't take her long once she got started.

She supported her arguments well, launching into chapter and verse about the lack of success of the death penalty as a crime deterrent and its adverse effects on society, quoting facts and impressive statistics about the number of innocent people who had been executed. She topped her discourse with, "Do you know that States with the death penalty have a higher murder rate than States without it?"

As she continued, Brad nodded attentively, from time to time interjecting a few comments. Actually, not really comments, more like polite utterances, the kind you make when you're holding up your end of a conversation that's really more like the other person's monologue. There's nothing specific they want you to say, yet they demand your attention. Brad sensed this about her and floated a few comments whenever he could slide one in, an occasional "Uh-huh," "Yes, right."

or "I see," showing he was listening attentively. When there was a little more space he offered, "You've got a point there...about that prof, I mean." As he thought about this, he figured what he should be saying was more like, "My God, get real! The guy's a confessed killer, a butcher." But something told him this wasn't the time.

Whatever his reasons, feeling off balance, he could not bring himself to disagree with her, not about capital punishment, not about anything. He sensed she would up and leave again. Besides, how could he possibly argue with a woman who was so breathtakingly beautiful? To him, it wouldn't be right...a violation of some natural law. Beauty was clobbering the Beast— nature's way of perpetuating the species—and he knew it.

It wasn't just her looks that attracted him. She seemed sure of herself and serious. Even so, he sensed that if he told her how he really felt, and unleashed full blast his well-rooted logic espousing the opposite point of view, he might very well bury her with rhetoric. Then he'd lose her before he even got to know her. He couldn't chance it. He'd change this approach after they got to know each other better, but not yet.

They slept together on their second date. The mutual attraction was undeniable. The night was surprisingly powerful and satisfying for both of them, a magnificent release, a life-altering experience that seemed to indicate the promise of a future together. Three months later they decided to share an apartment for the rest of their time in Gainesville.

During this getting-to-know-each-other-better time they had many stimulating conversations. A grad student, he was especially knowledgeable in literature and history and working on his MFA in Creative Writing. She apparently appreciated his clever wit and insightful writings.

"You know, Brad," she said one day, "you've got great potential. I'll bet you're going to be a famous writer someday, especially if I coach you along the way."

"Oh, really? Think I need coaching?"

"Two minds are better than one."

"If you just do your law thing well, I'm sure that'll be wonderful. That'll be enough for me. Then I can concentrate on the writing."

She responded with a smile.

They admired each other's attractive looks as well as their scholastic standing and delighted in showing each other off at campus parties. They were university *who's who* types, popular, winsome. Not only matched intellectually, they continued to escalate their physical relationship. The way they touched each other with such commitment and sincerity seemed to confirm their belief in the potential strength of a superior relationship, full of hope and admiration, propelled by the mutual attraction of achievement and importance.

Unfortunately, Brad soon found he could not prevail in any discussion with Jennie whenever they had opposite points of view—politics, the economy, foods. She pressed her arguments until he no longer cared about persuading her. The issues never seemed that important to him. She had a way of keeping score, like some women can do long after the game is over, which he didn't understand. It irritated him.

Anxious to keep the peace, he avoided confrontations with her. He remained convinced the least he could do with the woman that dazzled him was to deflect serious argument and prevent unpleasant collisions. But this apparent diffidence was more deeply rooted. He just didn't trust himself to be frank with her, even if he wanted to, and struggled to keep control of himself. He was concerned that if he were provoked far enough, he might unleash a darker aspect of his character … his violent temper.

One day she surprised him with, "Bradley, I don't like the way you weasel around when we have a serious discussion, like you did two weeks ago when we were talking about the rent. Why don't you come right out and say what you think, the way you do when you write your editorials?"

"You always say that. I've told you. I don't like arguing with you."

"Well your writing is brilliant. You express yourself well in your editorials, but I never know what you're thinking."

"Then read the paper, heh, heh."

"You sonavabitch. You know what I mean. Why don't you ever level with me?"

Where did that come from? Whew. "I guess because maybe I don't think you can take the truth."

"What do mean by that?"

"Every time we have a discussion, you get pissed if I disagree with you."

"Oh really?"

This was the perfect opportunity for him to tell her the truth. It was risky, but it would clear the air. Instead he paused, then said, "Look, honey, I love you, and I'm lucky to have found you. I just don't want to bicker. Please don't get me started."

"Grow up, Brad. This is a relationship. Speak you mind."

"Just trying to keep the peace. I'd really appreciate it if we could drop it now. Let's not argue over something stupid."

"Are you saying I'm stupid?"

"No, of course not."

"Well, that's what you implied."

"I don't think I did."

"Well, you did. And I don't appreciate it. What right have you to call me stupid?"

"Sorry."

"My reasoning powers are at least as good as yours and my class ranking is, as a matter of fact, higher than yours. So your assigning that appellation to me is entirely off base."

Brad struggled not to get angry, but he was getting hot. He said softly and carefully, "Jennie, you know what? You're right. It was a misunderstanding, a careless remark. I'm really sorry."

Jennie glared and didn't talk to him for a week. He couldn't stand it.

A few weeks later they made love one night after having dinner and wine at an inexpensive little Italian restaurant. It was his birthday. She gave him his present that night with complete abandon. Wounds were healed. Egos were salved. Once again they were on a smooth course. Brad was especially careful how he phrased his opinions. He hated it when she was unhappy with him and felt it was within his power to control the situation— just don't let her start up.

They married a year later, a typical post-graduation, garden-and-flowers event with hundreds of friends toasting the high-profile bride and groom. There seemed to be no limit to what they could accomplish in the future.

Brad and Jennifer relocated to Miami where they had found positions in their chosen professions. The new environment had its own challenges. Florida's largest metropolis, over three hundred miles to the south, whirled with a maze of diverse cultures. Many people barged though their daily lives fueled with the peculiar arrogance of ethnic self-absorption.

For those who could adapt, Miami was a stimulating land of possibilities, offering outstanding opportunities for the ambitious. This proved to be so for Brad and especially for Jennie.

She applied herself diligently to her work as an attorney with the firm of Bender, Slather and Schwartz. She made partner after five years. Brad told her it was an amazing achievement. She had built a reputation with brilliant pretrial and courtroom work. She already had an impressive reputation as counsel in major crime cases. Her career was on a fast track.

They lived in an expensive South Beach high-rise condo with spectacular views—the ocean to the east and Biscayne Bay and the city on the opposite side.

Brad appreciated his position teaching in the Creative Writing Department at Florida International University in North Miami. He loved it and it gave him time to write. A few of Brad's stories had been published in literary magazines and he was nearly finished with his second novel—the first, a tale about the gentility of the Old South, was a dud.

"What are you working on now?" Jennie asked one day.

"It's a novel based on a cruise director who runs a prostitution racket for passengers in Caribbean ports-of-call and gets murdered onboard ship."

"Really? Sounds trashy. Think this one will get published?"

"I've sent out the synopsis. Already gotten publisher interest. Looks good."

"There's not much sense in writing a book unless it gets published, you know."

"I know."

Like many Florida writers Brad had decided to set the new novel in steamy South Florida, ala *Miami Noir*, which had become a trendy market for crime fiction, rich in larger-than-life stories. One had only to read the Miami Herald to find inspiration for a yet another bizarre who-murdered-whom. For good writers it didn't take much to turn these into fiction. There was an eager audience for this stuff.

"You write so well. But if that's what you're going to do, why don't you do a textbook on writing? It could get published by the University and you'll have built-in sales for years."

A fair suggestion. But he sensed another issue. "I want to write fiction, not textbooks."

"Everybody writes fiction," she said. "Most of it gets lost in the crowd. The smart thing is to follow the money trail and the success odds. Textbooks last and have a guaranteed high-price market. Sure, they screw the students, but that's the way it is. My God, for the life of me, I don't know why you don't see that? What are you afraid of? After all, you're just writing words, so why not write ones that pay off?"

"Damn it, Jennie! Why the hell don't you let me handle my career my way? Why do you keep trying to boss me around? I'm frigging sick of it!" As soon as he said it he knew his temper was bubbling up and could get a lot worse. He also knew he'd pay for the outburst.

She glared at him with *that look* and stormed out of the room. He got the chill treatment, this time for a month. She didn't talk to him except when she had to, and started staying late at her office.

Eventually their stand-off ran its course and life seemed to settle back to normal. Jennie was still the most beautiful looking woman in the world to him, and even though they continued love-making, in a fashion, he knew they were heading for serious trouble. Whether it was their jobs, the fast-paced environment, not being under the umbrella of Gainesville's small-town culture, or something else, the fabric of their relationship was picking up unraveling-speed.

At first Brad blamed it on their careers. They rarely spent time together now. No more art films every two weeks, no more quickie trips to the Bahamas for weekend escapes. No more arts and crafts shows in Coconut Grove. They had become more interested in their work than in each other.

He saw the communication crevasse widening and tried to bridge it by backing off future arguments completely. But the fact that Jennie made over three times as much money as Brad had a negative effect on both of them. She grew more assertive; he, more reticent.

"Why aren't you working on your Doctorate?" she asked one day. "How are you ever going to be head of the department without a Doctorate?"

"I've told you before, I don't want to be the head of the department. I like teaching and writing. It suits me. A person should do what makes him happy."

"Well, you should get your Doctorate. It'd be better for your reputation. You're wasting your time teaching when you could be in charge of the program."

"I don't want to do that."

"I don't see why not. Rachael's husband is Director of Operations for the cruise line now. He went to school nights to do it."

"I went to school long enough."

"You lack ambition."

"That's really not it."

"Bullshit. If you had any pride you'd push yourself ahead."

He was about to blow. But he restrained himself and said, "Alright, alright. Whatever you say. I'll start working on it after the winter semester. Please let's not talk about this anymore."

That night they didn't make love. Instead they had aggressive sex without speaking, using each other like one-nighter strangers who would never see each other again. When it was over, there were no miracles. No magic. No love. No satisfaction. What remained was the emptiness of impersonal desire temporarily gratified. Months passed with no further physical contact.

One evening when they were home at the same time, the phone rang. "Hello?" Brad said, then listened for several minutes. Finally he spoke again. "Well, turkeys don't vote for Thanksgiving, you know."

He heard his brother say, "What's that suppose to mean?"

"It means why are you still seeing that woman when you know she's destroying you. She'll chop you up."

"I'm trying to break it off, but I can't," his brother said.

Brad moved to the foyer. "You've got to, Andy. You're a wreck. Anybody can see that. She's doing you in. You don't see her for a few weeks and you begin getting yourself together. Then she calls, and it starts all over."

"But I love her," Andy whined, "I know I shouldn't, but I do."

"Andy, you're my brother. I care about you. I'm telling you, it's going to end up bad. I can feel it coming."

"She's just confused."

"*She's* confused? Get a grip. Cut out, man."

"You don't understand," Andy pleaded, "it's not that simple."

"Andy, break it off before you do something rash. Don't let that happen."

"I gotta hang up now."

"I'll check with you in a few days, Andy. Listen to what I'm telling you."

"Okay, okay."

Brad hung up the phone. Jennie did not look up; apparently she hadn't been listening. She was curled up on the living room couch, legs tucked under her, concentrating on a deposition she'd brought home from the office. From time to time she marked a section with a yellow highlighter.

Brad eased open the sliding glass doors and stepped out onto the balcony. He stared into the night and thought about his brother. He was afraid he'd do something he'd regret if he didn't get free of that woman.

His gaze fixed across Biscayne Bay. The downtown Miami skyline dazzled like an amusement park. The National Bank building, formerly Centrust Tower, was lit up as usual. Tonight its wide bands of orange and green lights reminded everyone the University of Miami Hurricanes football team was playing in the Orange Bowl.

Sometimes the fifty-story building was illuminated red, white and blue, depending on the season or holiday. Brad's favorite was Valentine's Day red—the thought of which brought him back to reflecting on his brother's predicament. Poor fool, in love with a woman who's really bad for him, and too weak to do something about it. *I'd hate to be in his shoes.*

He joined Jennie in the living room. After a few moments she said, without looking up from her work, "Well, you certainly have strong feelings about your brother's life. What on earth was that all about?"

"I can't for the life of me see why, when Andy knows he's in a destructive relationship, he doesn't do something about it."

"Some people choose to hang on to things that were once something else," she said. Brad ignored the implication. "Does she have a name?" she added.

"Shirley, I think."

"Where does she live?"

"A trailer park up in Jensen Beach, past Stuart. She's got a couple of kids. Andy gives her money to help her out."

"What do you know about her?"

"Andy brought her into town once and introduced her to me at the college. She's got a sexy body for sure, really built, but no class. She's foul-mouthed, for one thing. She's just dangling him. He's continually upset. She knows how to manipulate him. It's all about sex, I'm sure."

"Why doesn't he just confront her and tell her to clean up her act. She'll never respect him if he doesn't stand up to her. If he really loves her, it's the least he can do."

"Maybe he's afraid he'll lose her."

"He won't keep her like that." A protracted silence followed. "What else, Brad?"

"For one thing, she has those ugly tattoos all over her arms. What is it with that stuff, anyway? That's why Andy has that upside-down cross on his left forearm; it's just like hers. That crap is for kids...or Neanderthals."

"Are you serious? What's wrong with tattoos? Really, you can't fault her for having tattoos. Where have you been? I can't believe you're so behind the times. Lots of women have them. Movie stars, teachers, models, nurses, athletes...everybody has them."

"Yeah, but not all over them."

"What the hell's the big deal? I was thinking about getting one myself."

"Where?" Brad bit the bait. She appeared to be waiting for his reaction. He sensed a disagreement coming that could turn his tattoo remarks into a major confrontation. The conversation was heading toward quicksand. He didn't think their relationship could handle another one. He wished he hadn't brought up the subject.

"Where?" she echoed. "Maybe on my thigh. Maybe a bumblebee or a flower. Or maybe a dagger? It'd be fun, don't you think?"

"Oh, please, Jennie. Far be it from me to interfere in your life, but that's disgusting."

"Nothing like a little honest communication, I always say. But as usual, you're just being chauvinistically judgmental."

"Jennie, if you want to get one, go ahead. I just don't like them on women."

"Nothing wrong with tattoos," she said. "Besides, I don't need your permission. It's my body."

"That's not the point."

"It *is* the point. Give me one good reason not to have a tattoo."

"Jennie, you're a lawyer in a respected law firm. How would that look? Is that the professional image you want?"

"Who would see it? Nobody but me. Don't you get it? It's for me. If I want to decorate my body a little, there's nothing wrong with that."

"What is this, the Fourth of July? You want to decorate yourself like the National Bank building?"

"Ho, ho. And what do you call lipstick? Mascara? Makeup? Women have been decorating themselves for thousands of years. Men seem to like it."

"Oh come on, that's not the same. You know what I mean."

"The principle is the same."

Brad was pressing, but tried one more point. "Well, what about on vacation or at the pool?"

"Yeah, so?" She waited for his response. As usual she had been tireless in rebuttal.

He shook his head and shut down. He knew he would say something he'd be sorry for. He didn't want to live with that again. It had been a long day. The discussion was over.

The next night before dinner she started in with, "I think you're being entirely unreasonable about tattoos. What right have you to decide what is …"

"Hold it, Jennie. I just was telling you how I felt about it. I thought you'd want to know."

"You weren't telling me. You were pontificating, dictating, like only you know what's right for women. What kind of intelligent enlightenment is that?"

"Oh, forget it."

"I won't." They ate by the TV and hardly spoke, as ABC News scoured the world for the day's most unpleasant news.

Brad missed the physical tenderness they once shared. Sex had always been a way of allowing their flawed relationship to be tolerable. But it had been many months now. For a long time he kept hoping the old affectionate Jennie would reappear, but after awhile he didn't care. The once-dedicated lovers focused mostly on their own wants and each other's faults.

Once, when he withdrew from an intense discussion, she apparently sensed his mood and said, "Don't be so sensitive. We're just talking, you know."

"Yeah sure, right." Debating is more like it, he said to himself. At times like this, he usually retreated to the den to write or bury himself in his work critiquing students' papers. He felt more and more worthless in her eyes, no longer respected. The alienation festered.

In classes, however, Brad was king of the hill. He was extremely popular with his students. His youthful good looks and enthusiasm mesmerized them. More importantly, he listened to them, creating a symbiotic rapport. He felt he knew each one personally and spent extra hours helping them work on writing problems, an ideal creative writing teacher-student relationship. It was the kind of bond he enjoyed. They loved him. He was respected, appreciated. As a result, his classes were less formal than the average university class, and certainly more rewarding for the students.

Some time later he proposed a question to one of his advanced classes, a precocious group of fifteen bright minds he found particularly stimulating, "How many of you women have tattoos?"

For a moment there was silence. Glances darted about. One guy murmured, "All of them." About half the women quickly raised their hands. A few more put up theirs. Then most all of them did.

One spoke up and said it was a woman's right to have tattoos all over her if she wanted to. It was her body. Period. Others chimed in. All seemed to agree.

"Okay, you've made your point; you like tattoos. I can see that. But what's the attraction? You're in your prime. Your skin is God-given lovely. Why spoil it? You're desecrating it just for a fad. What if you change your mind later? Look at it this way: a tattoo is like writing fiction where your protagonist has a *character defect*. Once he has it, he has it. It doesn't go away."

"Brad, you're pretty old-fashioned for a contemporary guy," said Patti, an attractive grad student in her mid-twenties. "What's the big deal? Look at it this way. It's my body. If I choose to get a tattoo, I'm in charge of me. Maybe it 's contrary to the mores of past generations. But now is now. And that's the fun of it. I can do it, so I do. And it's really nobody's business but mine."

The class cheered.

Hellooo. A gong clanged in his belfry. The message was clear. These women had clearly stated their case, different from his, and he wasn't offended. Their arguments made absolute sense to them and to him too. He didn't feel abused or dominated. Why couldn't he have that kind of exchange with his wife? Was he just too sensitive? Yes, maybe. It occurred to him that crossing the tattoo-bridge to his wife's side might be a way to begin mending their relationship, even though it meant agreeing with her. But this time, really agreeing. It would show her he wasn't so set in his ways. He'd tell her he didn't give a damn whether she got a tattoo or not. Just like she said … it was her body. And while he was at it, he'd clear the air once and for all and tell her exactly how he felt about her haranguing him. Maybe that's just what she needed from him. If *he* could change, so could she. Who knows, maybe they might even capture some of their old passion. But from now on she would have to meet him half way.

After class ended that day he took his time stuffing his books into his briefcase, reflecting on what had just occurred. He felt more positive than he had in a long time, renewed, buoyant. Ilona, one of his students, younger than the others, lingered after the rest of class left. She shut the door carefully, turned and walked back to Brad's desk.

"Can you come to my place tonight?" she said. "I'm feeling horny." She smiled coyly, then closed her eyes, wrapped her arms around herself and wriggled slowly, moving her head side to side, her long blonde tresses flouncing like a Pantene commercial.

"Ilona, stop. Listen to me. I'm sorry, but I can't see you anymore. I just can't."

"What? Why? What did I do? I don't have tattoos. You said you really cared for me."

"I do. But you know I'm married. I never should have started with you. I'm sorry. But I can't continue."

"That's not fair. What am I supposed to do? Stop loving you?"

"I thought my wife and I were going to separate. But something has happened and I've got to try to keep the marriage together. That's all I can say."

"Yeah, sure. I get it. I could tell by the way you were looking at Patti today. You have eyes for her don't you? I know you. You want to screw her."

"That's not it at all. I've told you the truth. It's over, Ilona. I'm sorry."

He knew he could be in serious trouble if Ilona chose to tell anyone about them. At the very least, he could be fired. The goodtime era of prof-perks with impunity with women students had ended long before he began teaching. Times had changed. Maybe Ilona would take this further but he didn't think so. She was more the type to move on quickly to someone else. Their relationship was never about love or companionship or writing or the future. If she decided to talk to the administration, he'd have to deal with it.

As Brad finessed his way toward downtown on a busy I-95 late that afternoon, headed for the condo, he noticed the sky darkening over Miami. A typical summer thunderstorm was moving in from the west. He didn't care. He headed east on the Julia Tuttle Causeway to Miami Beach. For the first time in months he was anxious to get home.

He should have ended his affair long before. Sex had been easy and comfortable with Ilona but not inspiring like it used to be with Jennie. Ilona was certainly no Jennie. Jennie was smart, quick, beautiful. But Ilona didn't put any demands on him, and they never argued or even dated, just screwed each other's brains out in her apartment without complication, or so it seemed. But he saw it now for what it really was, an escape. He had to try to recover his marriage. With Andy's predicament compounding things, he realized family mattered most to him, his wife included. He had been wrong about some things for so long. He knew he had to change. He hoped it wasn't too little too late.

Before Jennie got home, Brad noticed the names of a few South Beach tattoo inkers on a desk pad. He looked them over and decided to write Jennie a note.

Hi honey, I'd be glad to go with you if you'd like, when you get your tattoo. You should have one. Just because I disagreed doesn't mean I don't love you. Me.

When she arrived he planned to discuss the tattoo issue with her again in light of his new resolve. He would be polite, yet as tireless as she was in discussion. He wouldn't let himself be intimidated, nor would he lose his temper.

In the distance, thunder rumbled intermittently like phantom freight cars crossing a trestle. From the 17th floor of his building he could see the storm approaching the city across the bay. The tall white and gray buildings, silhouetted against a darkened sky to the west, appeared paralyzed, resigned to imminent attack. He knew that soon the storm would envelop downtown, black it out, sweep east across the Bay and slam against the high-rises at the tip of South Beach. He looked forward to it. It was the kind of vicarious excitement he enjoyed, sound and fury, lots of action, drama; but he didn't have to feel responsible or take issue with its pros and cons.

It was not yet dark when Jennie arrived, just ahead of the storm. Brad, in his starting-over positive-thinking mode, wanted first to tell her all about his 'tattoo class', then explain how he was going to change. When she went into the bathroom, he opened a bottle a chilled of Sauvignon Blanc, plucked two wine glasses from the rack and poured generously. He knew her law practice could be stressful and it showed on her tonight. Perhaps the approaching weather combined with a cozy drink together might develop into something more significant. As absurd as he knew it was, he could even see them slipping into bed together later if everything went well, as if wine and weather could suddenly warm a relationship chilled by habit. The dreamer in him focused on this possibility and fueled his enthusiasm.

"Jennie, let me tell you about this class I had today," he said, as he handed her a glass of wine.

"Not now, Brad."

"Tough day?" he asked.

"Bradley, we've got to talk."

"You're upset about that old tattoo business, huh? I'm sorry, honey. I'm so old-fashioned sometimes. I want you to know that I really don't mind if …"

"Brad, listen. It's not about that."

"Good, I was afraid you'd think I was …"

"Brad. Please! I have something important to tell you."

"Okay, sorry, go ahead."

They walked into the living room, she lead the way. A silent procession of two, one determined, the other expectant. The only sound was the clicking of her heels on the hardwood floor. She sat down on the couch, set her glass on the coffee table and placed her palms on her knees, one ankle folded behind the other, like a finishing-school girl. Brad plopped into the leather easy chair and slugged down some wine.

They sat in quiet for a long minute. "So?" he said.

"Here it is," said Jennie, gathering a breath. "I've been seeing someone for a while. It's serious. I can't keep lying to you. I think we should consider a divorce."

"What?" He sat upright, set his wine on the end table and leaned forward. "What are you talking about?"

"We live like brother and sister, and not happy ones at that. Nothing like it was when we started out. And you're buried in your writing anyway. I just don't want to spend the rest of my life like this."

Brad felt the blood rush to his head, thump his temples. He was speechless. The wind picked up. The sky was darkening.

"Come on, Bradley, say something. What do you want to do? I'd like to know now, if you wouldn't mind."

"Okay. I, ah ... well, what do *you* want to do?" he asked.

"I just told you. Weren't you listening?"

Distant lighting strobed against the living room wall as the outer fringes of rain reached the condo.

"I want us to stay married," he said.

"Like this? No way. I know what's been going on with you and the young chippies in your classes. You're fucking them. You think I'm blind?"

Brad looked at the leather sandals on his bare feet, thought how comfortable they were, how simple and uncomplicated. Then he said quietly without raising his eyes, "There was only one, and that's over."

"As far as I'm concerned, that's what finally forced me to go outside our marriage for an affair...with a man I can relate to."

"*I* forced *you*? Which came first the chicken or the egg?"

"Don't get cute."

"Let me ask you this. Did you marry the person I am, or one you thought I'd be someday?"

"You just stopped growing. Not what I bargained for."

"I don't talk about some things because you'll only disagree with me. You don't care very much for what I have to say."

"That's bullshit, and you know it. You have a ready smile for strangers and conversations with everyone but me ... acquaintances, friends, waitresses, anyone but me. You don't take a take a stand on anything I'm interested in. If we're not talking about your writing or your books or your brother, there's no conversation. Even then, you end up patronizing me."

Brad understood and felt at fault again. He was losing ground. "Maybe you're right. Maybe I have done that sometimes. Truth is, I just didn't want to upset you."

"Well, that sure as hell has worked, hasn't it?"

"What I mean is ..."

"Yeah, I know what you mean." Jennie jumped on his comment.

He was sinking fast. And then he said it. "Look, Jennie, if you want a divorce, okay, if that's what you really want. But let's not *argue* about it, okay?" He was sweating. His temples banged like cymbals. He touched the sides his head and could feel the blue and purple veins swelling.

"No you don't," she said. You're not running away from this. We're not talking about capital punishment. We're talking about us."

"I know that."

"Face it, Brad, you're gutless." She paused to let her remark take hold. "That's just what you are; and what's more, you know it. You can be as spineless as your brother being involved with a low class tramp. He ought to know better. It's disgusting. I thought you'd change. Well, you haven't. If you want to wallow down there, fine. But I've had it. How can I respect you? You have no ambition except to write more meaningless drivel."

Driving rain pelted the glass doors. Jennie's taunts found their mark. He winced as the words stung like hornets over and over. He felt worthless. He knew she was right. Around her, and only her, he was a wimp. Useless. It had always been so. He didn't want it to be. No one else affected him like she had. He used to love her so much, yet now he hated her for it. Neither of them could change what they were. Like tattoos. They are what they are. And now she was having an affair and dumping him. Dumping *him*! Impossible. How could that be? His head spun, turning crimson. Bitch!

He got up from the chair next to the couch, took a few steps, squeezed his eyes shut as if to clear his focus. Slowly he shuffled a full circle. His ears rang with dissonance. He stopped, took root in a place, stared at the polished inlaid floor. He tilted his head to one side, obliquely admiring the smooth connectivity of the interlocking boards, envying their perfect harmony. Not moving his head from that angle, he raised his eyes and found her watching him with an imperious glare, her arms folded in front of her. He looked at her without expression. He could see it was over. Past the point of any verbal solution.

Even like this she was a beauty, perfect face, perfect figure. He had to agree with himself on this, nodding a few times in affirmation. But it no longer made any difference.

It was just two steps to the end table. Brad picked up the heavy, marble-based lamp, considering its heft as he lifted it. Turning the lamp around slowly he saw its faux-Grecian details without really looking at them. He faced his wife with a vacant gaze. He flexed his arm slightly, as if reconsidering the weight of the lamp. He had little doubt as to its possible effectiveness.

A slash of lighting shattered the sky, scattering down to the water. The thunder crack that followed was so close it appeared attached to the flash of millions of volts. The concurrent concussion shook the building, filled the apartment. Brad felt the impact pound into his testes, as if they were bulged by an internal hydraulic hammer. He weakened then steadied himself.

Rain sheeted against the glass. Whitecaps churned the chop in the bay. The fury of the storm was magnificent. If it had been music it might have been the surreal climax of a violent symphony—hammering percussion, choirs of brass stabbing and ricocheting, woodwinds and strings cascading, filling every sound crack, lest even a nano-second of silence escape un-orchestrated. The din excited him.

A thought too absurd to consider seriously swirled in his head. Yet there he was, looking at the lamp in his hands, measuring its suitability to perform a task other than its intended function. He liked the weight of it, the heft of it, the feel of it in his hands. It surrendered to him like the trust of a small pet. At last he was totally in control of the moment, of life, of her, of them.

For a moment he recalled the morning he and Jennie first met in Gainesville. There before him was the newspaper headline that had stimulated their meeting: *KILLER PROF GETS DEATH PENALTY*. Maybe the guy had to do it. But *still*, he did have a choice.

Brad stood motionless as the storm pounded. Jennie's eyes were fixed on the lamp. Her distain gave way to one wide-eyed terror. Her mouth opened in disbelief. He nodded to no one in particular, as if recognizing an inner voice and assenting to its direction. He stared at the lamp again. A new power suffused him, as though he had a premonition of what he would do. He had no doubts.

He turned to her with a sardonic smile and paused. For a moment all was silent. He let the silence ring, then placed the lamp carefully back on the table, taking his time straightening its shade with both hands, making sure its symmetry was in proper alignment and that it was restored to its former position, as if it had never been moved. He smirked. Without looking at her he walked out of the room, into his den, and closed the door.

**

Bird of Paradise...
*Miami Slice*_____

By the time I hustle though the terminal to the parking garage elevator and press the *up* button, I am dripping. Sweat trickles inside my shirt like reverse osmosis. It's sweltering today in Miami and the plane's defunct air conditioning didn't help. Felt like I was trapped inside a can.

The flight was only thirty minutes late. Could have been worse. Glad I didn't have baggage, just a briefcase. Waiting to claim luggage in Miami International takes almost as long as the flight from Orlando ... if you're lucky.

I take the empty elevator, which could have easily accommodated thirty people (or a Volkswagen Bug). It takes its time chugging up to the parking level. The stairs would have been quicker. The door at the other end of the box opens. I step out into the hallway. No AC.

147

I make my way though sliding glass doors to the moving walkway.

Perspiring like a steam-fitter, I finesse myself onto the rubber track of the moving walkway and stop. Let it perambulate for me. Rest and mop up time. Great invention, this walkway. I wipe my face and neck, slip the handkerchief inside my shirt for a few quick up-and-down chest passes.

In the distance a man is approaching from the opposite direction. I hurry. Convergence is imminent. I make one more pass. First one side then the other. A couple of extra dabs in the pits—they sop like a swamp. That will have to do. No more time. I start dripping again almost as soon as I stop.

As we pass each other (he on his own track) I turn away, managing an overt cough. I don't know if he noticed me mopping up. Wouldn't want him to think I had no class, even if he is a stranger. But there is such a thing as manners. I like to think so, anyway. I'm pathetic sometimes.

Is this walkway moving particularly slow today or is it just me? I start strolling, bouncing along with its rubber lift, taking long, loping strides, which increases the distance covered with each step. The sensation feels like I'm walking on the moon in slow motion. Not that I've been on the moon, of course. But, well, it feels that way. At the end of the moving ramp I am launched out into the open garage. Whatever cool air effect I've created by moving faster, stops when I do. The air is surly with tropical heat. But this *is* home and I'm glad to be here.

I locate my car on Level 4. It must be 120 degrees inside. An oven. I slip the key into the ignition and start it up. It's good to be in control of my own environment again. I am the captain now, pilot in command ... of my own car. Buckle up. The air conditioner goes on —hot air plunges out from the vents. I let the engine warm up to cool down the air. Ah, here it comes. That's better. Now that I think about it, why does the engine have to get hot to produce cold air? I know it does, sure. But why? Seems strange. Oh, forget it. I don't have time today to postulate theory on Air Conditioning 101. It's cooler now and that's all I need to know.

I work the car though the various parking levels toward the ground floor. The tires screech and scrunch each time I make a slow turn at the end of each short straight-a-way. The sound might be informing me the tires are too soft—but I know they're not. Or I'm going too fast. At ten miles an hour? Hmm. It's not as if I'm slow-driving up North on a frigid snow-packed road at night in a quiet suburb. That sure makes your tires scrunch, especially when you turn. But why should tires complain on smooth, freshly painted parking garage ramps? Oh well, life is full of cause-and-effect contradictions. Hot makes cold; smooth makes squeaks. Hmm, I'll have to think about that sometime.

I need to get to my office and finish a report before I go home. I'm taking my wife out to dinner—our usual Friday night date. If all goes well I'll make it in time. So far I'm almost on schedule. I'm at the exit level now, getting closer to the collection booths. The line seems to have stalled. I round the last bend and see why.

Only one of the three booths is operating and the Latina attendant is taking her sweet time making change for a driver. Just what I need. Come on now, really. She looks more interested in bantering with the perspiring amigo leaning into the other side of her booth—another attendant, I presume from the way he's dressed. I'm now close enough to hear them jabbering loudly in Spanish. Except for his hat, the guy could pass for a caricature of a mustached *Frito Bandito*—disheveled, officious, smiling juicily (seems to me) like the sleazy leader of a gang riding into town on horseback. Well, maybe not quite. But I wonder if he's been inspired by those old Tex-Mex movies? Or maybe the movies have seen him.

Frito's wrinkled khaki shirt has green cloth shoulder epaulettes. The shirt is almost tucked into loose jeans, which are cinched with a wide belt just below his undenied belly. He wears a green cap, under which a crop of un-mown black hair straggles out at the sides.

I feel like I just landed back in time … in Juarez, or Laredo, the era of *The Magnificent Seven*. "Give me de gold and your woman, hombre, or I will keel you."

Resigned to a scene over which I have no control, I wait for them to finish chattering. My mind wanders off into nebulous strata, unfocused, and decides to enjoy an out-of-body experience, a little daydream. Maybe I'll contemplate air conditioning. May as well make some use of the time. Isn't that what daydreams are for? My mind lolls into a semi-dazed escape, but my glazed eyes remain fixed on the two attendants, as if attached to them by some invisible conduit through which we would instantly connect as soon as they stop talking.

The car ahead of me moves.

Dream over.

I refocus.

La Latina collects a toll. Ah, progress. Then once again she pauses to converse with *El Frito*. It's amazing to me that she doesn't seem at all affected by the line of waiting cars. As a matter of fact, her behavior belies any trace of intimidation.

Trying to distract myself from doing or saying something stupid, I'm ready to escape into another mental blur. But wait, something penetrates my cloud. Something out of sync catches my eye. Something about her. It's not her lipstick, though the slathering of vermilion splashing her lips—the lip line presenting no natural barrier for the application—is not exactly out of the pages of *Vogue*. From the way she applies makeup I imagine she would have a difficult time trying to paint-by-number.

But that in itself is not the mood breaker. No. Like her friend she wears a khaki Parking Authority shirt with green epaulettes. Her blouse is as tight as the cover of a baseball. And now I see what has caught my attention. Affixed to her breast pocket, by some sturdy device no doubt, is a large bright orange Bird of Paradise blossom.

I'm intrigued. This is crazy. This is fun. All right! A huge colorful flower sits atop one of the khaki hilltops like a Mayan oracle. I love the wildness of it, the what-do-I-care of it. Here is someone who enjoys being herself. Her unique expression of femininity says it all. Unsophisticated, true, yet it bears a certain panache, a necessary little personal aberration to cope with what I'm sure must be a mundane job. It's a colorful thread of the proud individuality evidenced by many of the burgeoning Hispanic culture in Miami. Hooray for her!

I've seen many different kinds of flowers pinned to blouses before, but I can honestly say this is my first encounter with a Bird of Paradise.

The green beak of its long blossom appears to be pecking at her neck as she turns back and forth from her register collecting tolls. At various times she swings to the other side, toward her story-telling visitor, laughs heartily, then returns to her register, resuming her duties. Duties? Well, sort of. These interruptions, of course, slow down the toll-taking process—especially irritating if you are in line and in a hurry. I am in both. Okay, folks. Enough already. Give me a break. Can't you see my positive feelings are deteriorating?

Cars ahead move.

I inch mine forward until I am next.

The line behind me grows longer by the minute. Just as I reach the right position for being duly processed, the smiling *Fam da Flor* again aborts her collecting duties. She turns away and faces her jabbering fellow worker. I say worker, though he has done nothing so far to verify that assumption. She lets out a long, high-pitched jangle of laughter, adding an animated, "*Ayee, ayee.*" Obviously, she is in no hurry to serve the public. Throwing back her head, she slaps at his arms repeatedly, shaking her head in approval of his presumably naughty story. I wish I knew the joke. I could use a good laugh.

The more she reacts, the more animated *Frito's* storytelling gets. There's nothing like a receptive audience to inspire a performer. His punctuating gestures become more expansive until the woman finally doubles over in laughter, cramp-like, clapping her hands together, almost unable to stand up. Now I worry she'll have to pee at any minute. That'll just mean an even longer wait. Come on you guys, knock it off. I'm waiting.

I watch intently for another minute or two—it seems like an hour—a captive of their sideshow.

Though I'm a bit envious of her exuberance, I am now irritated. So I try to intimidate them with an intense stare. I fancy myself a latter-day Svengali. My blue eyes try to burn daggers at them. I use my best get-tough focus. Enough already, it says, finish the story, get to the punch line.

No effect.

The giggling woman, now with her back to me, surely is aware of me, and the man avoids my attempt to make eye contact with him. He continues yakking while she-of-the-giggles obliges with more of the same. Now she's blowing her nose again and again. Why do people blow their noses after laughing or crying? I never do. Frankly I really don't care. One thing is certain, though. Even if I weren't in a hurry, I would be now.

I *beep beep* the horn of my BMW to get their attention. Would anyone blame me?

That does it. She swings around to collect my money, apparently shocked by the audacity of the horn. But in doing so her affixed Bird of Paradise catches the edge of her window, wiggles tenuously for a moment, then disengages completely from its perch, flopping out on to the pavement into the path of my purring Beamer. In disbelief she watches. Her eyes follow it as if it has traveled to the pavement in slow motion.

I can't resist. I rev up the motor, giving the accelerator a loud *vroom* ... but just once. Then quickly I offer her a friendly wave and an exaggerated smile through the windshield, as if to say, *only kidding, lady. I wouldn't run over your flower. Heh, heh.*

Suspecting, I would guess, that there is something disingenuous in this greeting, she glares razors at me. Her mouth tightens, her eyes squint. Her once-crimson-happy cheeks drain to ashen anger. A formidable woman, I'd say. Not to be trifled with. The party's over.

She alights from the booth, immediately blocks a hand out to me, as if an *importante* traffic cop were now in command. She assumes the demeanor of a public servant recently empowered by a minor municipally-appointed cousin.

She stiffens, issues a loud, *"Momento! Momento!"* Once amused by her *joie de vivre*, I am now offended by her arrogance.

Retrieving the large flower, she stands there, blowing on it then carefully brushes it off.

Suddenly, a cacophony of horns blares from behind me. The line of impatient motorists has apparently reached the end of its stretched-out fuse. Perhaps bonded by a common cause, fueled by the July afternoon heat and the tedious wait, a traffic jam session of impromptu chaos erupts. One horn seems to inspire another, like dogs barking in a neighborhood, until the whole parking garage is alive with car-barking.

Pigeons scatter from eaves. Passengers cover their ears. Drivers yell obscenities. The din must be heard for miles.

It's deafening. Yet in a way it's beautiful, a cacophonic symphony. I have allies. The voice of the people is rising in righteous indignation, without fear or favor, as if declaring its indisputable right-of-way, flower or no flower, like a giant freight train blaring its horn, bearing down on a rural crossing. Come on … out of the way! Move it or we'll mow you down. I like it.

You would think all this commotion would cause some token scurrying by the un-attending attendants. But no. *La Latina* still faces the man as he slowly eases away from the other side of the booth. Even as he back-pedals toward his unoccupied station, increasing the distance between them, he continues yelling out his story to her, laughing, gesticulating with undiminished vigor.

She obliges with continued giggling, watching him, waiting until he finishes and enters his toll booth. Only when he turns on the green light for his booth does she return to her register. Suddenly, she is all business. Her big smile drops away to somewhere below the equator. She makes a drawn-out ceremony of reorganizing and counting her money. The stalling is galling. It continues. So does the horn-blowing.

I stretch out my hand, holding the ticket and a twenty-dollar bill. She snatches them with a glare that issues a silent challenge: I'm in charge here and you are insignificant. I understand the look. I've seen it before. An acerbic retort from me would certainly be justified at this point, but a shouting exchange would only make things worse. It will hold me up longer, and it won't help the situation. So I ignore the this-is-my-turf challenge, but at the same time I lose all appreciation for her creative individuality. It's another example of the screwy cause-and-effect syndrome: making people angry because you're so happy.

I begin to dwell negatively on her conduct. She seems to sense it. After banging a roll of wrapped coins against the register and splattering its contents into the drawer, she finally deigns to make change, slapping, without a word, smaller bills, some change and a receipt

155

into my outstretched hand. Her squinting eyes glare at me.

Her rudeness is offensive. Perhaps a simple seven-letter two-word phase could have been called for. But then my crudeness would have equaled hers. I realize her belligerence is not typical. Many in the Latin community are embarrassed by such behavior and feel it reflects badly on them. I decide not to pursue the issue. I just want to get out of here. Let others confront her. Let them spoil their day.

In the few minutes I have observed her, the woman has transformed herself from a fun-loving soul, filled with esprit, to an onerously feisty bitch. Ah, we humans can be touchy when we have to do things we don't want to do. Especially in this heat.

Though I keep my cool, I consider things I could say as she gives me my change. *So where's the happy Senorita now? It's people like you that give Latinos in this city a bad name.* But I don't say that. Instead, I nod with an exaggerated smile and offer, "Gracias, Senorita, and Buenos Dias to you, too. WELCOME TO AMERICA!" I can't resist. At least I've said something. I wonder if she gets the point. Probably not. But I feel better. And that's important. I'm the one I have to deal with for the rest of the day. Why should I go around with a sour puss because of her? Life is what it is.

I pull away and drive out of the parking garage up onto the connector for Route 836 toward downtown. WELCOME TO MIAMI, a large sign announces as I leave the airport. Hmm.

In the last decades this once quiet tourist town has exploded into a sprawling multi-ethnic metropolis. South Florida's panorama now has a different perspective. The land of *Milk and Honey* of pre-Castro Revolution years has long since added black beans and rice to its metaphorical landscape. That's fine with me. Multi-culturalism has been great for the city. But it does have its moments. Like for instance, yielding the right-of-way when driving has become about as unpopular as using brakes. Oh, well, *c'est la vie.*

I make it to the office and get my report done. After I leave, I spot a curbside vendor selling flowers on Second Avenue under the overpass near the Rickenbacker Bridge to Key Biscayne. She's a smiling, pleasant woman, heavy set, holding out bunches of flowers to passing motorists. What the hell. I pull over. "Do you have any Bird of Paradise blossoms, Senorita? Big ones?" A teasing idea scenarios my tired, sick mind. Or is it just my sense of humor? Should I do it?

"Si, bee-yu-teeful. Two for fi dollah. One is beeg. One not so beeg, but very preetie."

"I'll take them."

I can't resist. I get home a little late. After setting down my briefcase, I give my gorgeous wife a warm kiss and a one-arm-hug. "My, don't you look beautiful tonight all dressed up already." She is wearing a tastefully fitted tropical sheath of subdued red, orange and tan circular patterns. A single strap sets off her lovely, tanned shoulders. Around her neck an elegant gold pendant graces the sinews of her delicately articulated clavicles. Beige and red leather heels complete her ensemble. To me she personifies the look of tasteful individuality. I stand back, look at her again. Yes, she is so balanced. So perfect. I am such a lucky guy.

I reach from behind me, present the two blossoms. "Carmen, honey, here … pin these on. They're the latest thing. Everybody's wearing them." Again, I can't resist.

She glances at the Birds of Paradise and gives me a you've-got-be-kidding look. Right away she knows my suggestion is a lame attempt at a joke. I figure she'll put water in a bowl and the birdies will enjoy a little swim. Then I'll tell her what happened at the airport this afternoon and we'll enjoy a good laugh.

But instead, she takes the flowers from me. "Sweetheart, you're so thoughtful."

Easing into the bathroom, not closing the door, she sets the flowers on the vanity. She stands before the mirror for a few moments studying herself. I watch as she brushes her lustrous, long dark hair with slow careful strokes, the way a woman does when she's thinking of something else. She turns, gives me a flirty eye and a wink, gathers her hair into a pony tail, clips it in place. After looking approvingly at herself, this way and that, she affixes the smaller bright orange flower onto the right side of her head. The larger one she places in a glass of water.

She checks herself in the mirror at all angles then sashays out, smiling, looking absolutely smashing. I am impressed. The intriguing blossom is mesmerizing, yet it doesn't compare with the fascinating flower who wears it.

"Okay, my *Gringo* wise guy," she says, "let's go out for Cuban tonight … then some dancing on South Beach."

**

The Beach...
Life After Pennsylvania_____

"So, you like that book, eh?" Paul said, as he wriggled back and forth in his webbed beach chair, trying to level it in the soft sand, trying to get comfortable, trying to make chit-chat about anything when he didn't really care one way or another about anything.

"Huh?" his wife said from her chair, not looking up.

"Do you like the book?"

"It's okay."

Paul sat back and looked out at the ocean. He wondered if oceans ever got tired of coming and going to the same places everyday. And if they did, did each globule of water have its own real estate to service? Or did it free lance, eventually traveling the world over thousands of millennia, visiting different places, never to return? Where did it start? Where did it end? Hmm.

Hey, he wanted to say to the ocean, what's with you, anyway?

He gazed along the almost deserted two-mile stretch of khaki-smooth sand, then out at the Atlantic. Wave after wave rolled softly onto the beach. He watched the gulls hover in mid-air, almost stationary against the steady breeze. The sun pressed against his body while at the same time cooling zephyrs were dueling to deflect the heat.

"Notice how much cooler it is here? I mean in comparison to how hot it was on the street?"

"Uh-huh," his wife said.

"That's called wind-factor, or more commonly, wind chill. For every knot of wind velocity, air temperature appears to decrease by about one degree."

No answer.

"It must be at least ten degrees cooler here on the beach because of the breeze, don't you think?"

"Right."

"That would mean the wind is blowing at about ten knots."

No response.

"Don't you love how I tell you everything I know?"

"Uh-huh."

"Even if I don't know stuff, I make it up, just for you," he said, almost chuckling. Then, "Well, I *am* trying to make conversation."

His wife looked up. "Why is it that whenever I pick up a book to read you decide to talk to me?"

"Whew. I think I'll go for a walk. See you later."

"Okay, sweetie. Bye."

He took a few barefooted steps in the pillow-soft sand then turned to her. "You say *sweetie*, but that's not what you really mean, is it? You mean *pain-in-the-ass*, right?"

"Right."

"Well, same to you, too."

"Oh, go soak your head."

"Right." Paul mushed through the hot sand until he was closer to the water where the beach was firm and damp. He liked it that way. Cool. Easy walking. He was in no hurry. After all, there was nowhere he had to go. No particular destination. If he were the ocean he'd just continue to mosey back and forth to the shore and enjoy the day.

Occasionally, front-reaches of a spent wave covered his feet before soaking into the sand or returning to the ocean. He could have easily hopped out of the way, if he had the energy … or cared. But the cool water felt good on his bare feet. For a moment it took his mind off his malaise, or loneliness, or whatever it was.

The water always intrigued him, but he had no desire to actually swim in it. Instead, when he walked the beach these days he imagined himself wading deep into waves that would push against his chest until eventually they covered his head. And when they did, he would keep walking along the smooth, sandy bottom, ever deeper, where it was darker and serene. Tiny multi-colored fish would dart between his legs and scurry about, happy to see him. Elephant-ear purple and green sea plants, delta-veined, would sway in unison to the ebb and flow of the invisible current, waving at him like exotic hula dancers undulating in slow motion. It was peaceful and beautiful there, a retreat from the indifference of the world.

When his reverie faded he continued walking. He had to admit that he couldn't figure out women, at least not his wife. "You never talk to me," she complained. And invariably, when he did talk to her, she said he was just blabbing and not sharing ideas. He couldn't win.

When the passion died early, their marriage evolved into a respectful partnership, each doing his or her part dutifully. They raised their children, worked, paid their bills, decorated their houses, babysat their grandchildren, argued, ate, slept, went to church, read the papers. But there was no romance and little affection now. Even his attempts to hug her in bed were met with feigned pleas of fatigue and yawns.

Some women tire of touching before men do. They act like hugging is a silly interruption … of what, he didn't know. Of course she was never like that with their grandchildren. Hell, no. They got plenty of affection. Certainly he loved them too. But not the way love is supposed to be in a marriage. Of course babies needed lots of love and attention. That was obvious. He didn't resent that at all. He guessed he should have gotten over the feeling of being discarded.

The older he got, the more he missed it—the touching, the warmth. What would it cost? It didn't mean they'd get into a hot and heavy scene that would turn out to be disappointing for her. No. Just a little passing tenderness is all he wanted. No big deal, right? But he was out of the affection club. Another part of his life gone. As far as he was concerned, nature really screwed up that detail in the divine plan. Well, so be it.

Lately he had begun to crave ice cream and sweets. Freudian substitutes for affection? His wife, the realist, the homemaker, the one who took care of practical matters, was efficient and content with her responsibilities. He was just coasting, resigned to his own indifference.

It all started when he was "separated" from his job at Monongahela Light and Power, forced to resign after thirty-five years. The bottom suddenly dropped out of his life. "You can't do this to me." He was devastated. He was sixty-four.

Where was he to go?

"That's the thanks you get for being loyal to the company," his wife said. "A lot they care about you. That ought to tell you something."

"You don't understand."

"Look, Paul, you've been moping for months. Get over it. You have to make an adjustment and get on with life. Plenty of people lose their jobs. It's not the end of the world. We're comfortable. We have the children and the grandchildren, and we all love you; you know that."

But that kind of love wasn't enough for him anymore. He could never discuss his emotional needs and feelings with her. Whenever he did try to share a particular concern, she'd have a pragmatic answer that made any further discussion moot. "Oh, don't be silly," she'd say. Estelle had a black and white approach to life, and to her credit, seldom seemed hesitant or confused. He knew his unhappiness, if that's what it was, was his problem to work out on his own.

Paul had supervised his division for fifteen years. He'd cut operational costs by twenty-two percent, improved man-hour productivity, almost eliminated absenteeism by implementing flextime. But most important to him, the safety record for consecutive days of accident-free man-hours in his division was the best the plant had known. His Training and Review Program was the reason. He was most proud of that.

For years the company had trusted him. And he had never let the company down. His was a fine record. That is, until a sudden ring of the telephone jarred Paul and his wife from sleep in the middle of a September night last year.

"Paulie, get to the plant quick," a voice said. "There's been an explosion." He dressed hurriedly. Raced to the plant, not stopping for traffic lights. Emergency vehicles were on the scene when he got there. Smoke and debris everywhere. Halted fire trucks, engines running, whitish-gray hoses crisscrossing the ground like snakes. Parked police cars and ambulances flashing blinding staccatos of light. More sirens approaching. Spewing hydrants. Spotlights glaring. Steam and smoke ghosting silhouettes of wreckage. Part of the plant seemed to have collapsed. But he couldn't see any fire.

"What happened?" he asked his foreman.

"Number two boiler blew. Took out the whole side of the North Wing."

"Anyone hurt?"

"They got ten guys out already. Maybe more in there."

"How the hell could this happen?" he said.

"Automatic override system must have failed."

"What about manual shutdown? Who's the systems monitor tonight?"

"Haronski," said the foreman. "I saw him earlier. He was late coming in. Didn't look too stable."

"Where's he now?"

"Haven't found him."

Some months prior the night crew had been drastically reduced. One man was now to cover the usual responsibilities for each team of two. Paul had argued against the cuts, but senior management prevailed. The night the boiler blew, Haronski was in charge of monitoring West Wing gauges alone. Another worker had noticed his head drooping sometime prior to the accident.

When the system redlined and both the automatic cut-off and compression releases had failed to engage, for some inexplicable reason, Haronski had not switched to manual override—the failsafe backup in the event of critical system malfunction.

The boiler's runaway pressure accelerated unchecked. And BOOM! Six men had been hospitalized with severe burns in the explosion. Haronski had been killed.

"Human error, directly attributable to Haronski's lapse in following established procedure, probably by falling asleep," so concluded the lengthy safety investigation report. But the corporate review committee had a different take. They suggested Paul "should have foreseen Haronski's fatigue, clearly a technical violation of management responsibility."

Paul assured corporate executives his actions were consistent with company safety policies and in its best interest. Safety was always his first concern. But the new management team was unyielding.

Later, Paul realized the truth. For some time now he had exceeded his job classification's salary range. This was a convenient opportunity for the company to bring in a younger replacement for less money. Thus the firm could continue with its real purpose: the relentless pursuit of reducing payroll costs to affect a more attractive bottom line. Paul was asked to resign. They would give him full severance, of course … of he didn't dispute their offer. And they would attach no incident report—*released for cause*—to his personnel file.

"This agreement is in our mutual best interest," they said. Forget thirty-five years of impeccable service, he thought. Forget loyalty. Forget performance excellence. Forget people. It was all just numbers. It was all about money. More money for people at the top. It wasn't fair. *How could they do this to me?*

His wife said he shouldn't care. He should take his settlement money and leave. They needed a vacation anyway, so that's what they had done. But he figured the company could have at least made him a temporary consultant or something, after all he had done for them over the years. It wasn't about the money for him.

The plant had been such a part of his life. He remembered how proud he was years ago showing his two young sons the giant turbines that whirled faster than the speed of sound, or so it seemed, powering the city with vital electricity, turbines he had overseen. The way he figured it, there wasn't a more necessary job in the whole county. His kids were grown now with families. He guessed they had their own job equivalents of giant turbines to show their kids.

Estelle had suggested they get away from Pennsylvania for an extended vacation in Florida. They rented a place in a trailer park on the east coast a couple of hours south of Daytona for their first full winter of sunshine and no snow. It was something to be proud of, he guessed, coming to Florida. But personally, he liked the snow just fine.

For Paul the park was a dreadful place, with incessant bingo, shuffleboard games, and loud, uninteresting people. He missed his friends at the plant.

He missed his life. His job had been his reason for being.

Estelle was a good woman, but she never seemed to understand his connection to his work. Florida was her agenda now. She insisted they relax at the beach these days. And for a while he figured why not. It was nice enough, getting tanned and healthy looking. But it was boring. There was little to do, nothing that really mattered. More than anything he missed being needed. He had become just plain unnecessary.

The seagulls had the best of it, he decided. They could swoop and dive and glide and hover, then dart away at any time they felt like it. Or just stop flying and coast in the wind for miles. Not bad. Must be nice, he thought.

He watched as one of the intrepid gulls cruising close to the water suddenly snatched a fish with its claws. Every moment of its life was an adventure. He recalled a line of a verse and said it aloud. *"In airy lightness and living depths, peace, creatures seek and find."* Evidently some poet had it all figured out.

Farther down the beach he noticed a well-tanned blonde woman in a white bathing suit, lying alone on a large blue blanket. Instinctively he tightened his stomach and quickened his step.

From this distance the woman reminded him of Suzanne. Why couldn't his wife be a little more like his young, blue-eyed assistant of the past few years? Suzanne always listened to him when he talked about wind factors and temperature and wind chill and things like that. Several times she remarked how observant and knowledgeable he was. *Bright girl. Very perceptive.*

She became a fine assistant and interesting to talk with. He often wondered what happen to her when he 'retired.' He heard she had left the company shortly thereafter. He'd never know. Unless, maybe.... Wait a minute. Was it possible? He looked at the blue blanket again and squinted to focus more clearly. No, it couldn't be. Could it?

As he got closer, he shaded his eyes, trying to identify the sleeping young woman. Indeed what a coincidence this would be. Yes! His heart beat a little faster. Imagine, his former assistant, here in Florida, right on this very beach. Did she know he was here? Had someone told her he was in Florida? She understood him. He could talk to her. It would be a sign. Instantly his mood elevated a notch.

When he was close enough to call out her name, hardly feeling the hot sand burning at his feet, he stopped, stared for a time, thinking what would be the best way to greet her. *Hi, Miss Pittsburgh. What are you doing on my beach?* Or, *My God, Suzanne, you're a sight for sore eyes.* No. Too corny.

She looked so marvelous in the bathing suit, sensuous, glistening, tanned skin softly blending in with the sand. He had never thought of her like this. How absolutely perfect. He gathered a full breath and was just about to call out her name. But ...

The Beach

It wasn't Suzanne. *Stupid to even think so. What was I thinking? Well, it doesn't really matter anyway; you can't change reality.* Probably for the best. His wife was right. He had to accept things as they are and get on with living.

Once more Paul looked at the gulls gliding in the cloudless sky. He scanned the quiet beach as far as he could see and reasoned that even the tiniest grain of sand had a purpose. Each supported the next grain, which in turn supported the next, *ad infinitem*. Each speck insignificant, yet playing a integral role in nature's plan. Must be nice.

He turned toward the sea, sucked in a long slow breath, absorbed the salt air, held it, stretched, then exhaled. Casually he strolled down to the water's edge. He paused, smiled with a relaxed yawn. Gulls squawked. Ocean foam lapped at his knees. Thousands of mini-lights twinkled as the noon sun sparkled the water's surface.

Paul strode into the gentle waves ... now up to his waist. Now chest high. *Welcome, Paul,* the ocean said, and soothed him with mothering coolness.

He kept on going.

No one noticed.

**

Return Of The Brave...
Texas Homecoming

Lyle Baker arrived on a dusty Greyhound bus.

"Cleo Springs," the driver announced, pulling the vehicle to a stop at the curb. The air brakes wheezed a tired exhale. "If you're getting back on the bus, be here in ten minutes. Don't be late."

Baker had no intention of boarding the bus again. He stepped down, out into the bright, unforgiving Texas sun—just as he remembered it—squinted to get his bearings and stretched a bit. He felt the weight of the heat on his shoulders, even as it pulsed waves from the hot pavement up to his face. He recognized the smothering heat, the kind of dry heat he knew only here. It felt like home.

The driver retrieved a long brownish green canvas bag from the storage underbelly, and slung it roughly on the ground next to the bus. Baker paid no mind; he knew it was his. He strolled over and picked it up.

171

Hoisting the duffle bag onto his shoulder, he walked a little unevenly along Main Street, passing through the small downtown area. The street was practically deserted, but of course it was Sunday afternoon; most everything was closed. Nothing to bring people to town on a dog day like today. Folks would be out at the lake sunning or cooling off in the water. Some would be snoozing at home in comfortable porch chairs, resting up to go back to work the next day.

Lyle was a trim man, less than thirty, looked a little older, medium height, a firm waist, solid shoulders, thick dark straight hair, and a fine, chiseled face with prominent cheekbones. Ladies would consider him handsome. He walked erect favoring his right leg somewhat.

During the time be was away he imagined the time when he returned home. Things never changed much in Cleo Springs when he was growing up, so he figured the town would be pretty much the same as when he left in 1941. In some respects it was—hot and quiet. But when he looked for familiar landmarks, he noticed a few surprising changes.

For one thing, the corner where Jessup's Pool and Billiard Emporium used to be was occupied by a Studebaker dealership, with different colored cars parked neatly in rows on the lot in front of the building. A big American flag drooped from a high flagpole. Triangular red, white and blue pennants were strung on a wire surrounding the lot.

Hell, he'd never even seen a Studebaker before. It looked to him like the back end could have been the front. No running boards either. Shaped like a Buick

Rogers space ship. And not just black or gray, either; they were all kinds of fancy colors.

Perkins 5 & 10 was gone. A Kresge's store filled its space. The new building had a shiny metal front with big picture windows. Across the top hung a large red and white metal sign: *K R E S G E' S*. *Folks sure couldn't miss that.* Thank goodness the Bijou movie house was still there. He spent many a fun Friday night at the Bijou and it made him feel good seeing it as it used to be, like an old friend who never grew up. Posters in front advertised *Abbott and Costello Meet The Invisible Man*. Why not, he figured, an invisible man.

Main Street was now a newly blacktopped road, wide and quiet, with plenty of angle parking spaces on both sides. A double white line, as big as you please, striped the middle of the road … led straight into town from the highway. Never needed those before. Wouldn't matter much to hot-rodders, he guessed. But maybe they'd like it.

Across the street he saw the familiar Cleo Springs Bank. It had a different name but still looked like a one-story brick fort with windows. He'd be there tomorrow.

Lyle spent the night at the old Fairfax Hotel. The room cost him three dollars, *with shower*. Felt good, too. He'd been traveling for weeks to get home. The next morning he showered again, shaved, put on a fresh shirt and pressed pants. He hadn't wanted to do even that much dressing up for some time. The fresh clothes gave him a sense of importance and sort of confirmed he should be here.

He managed to practice a half-smile in the mirror, though it didn't come easy. A quick nod to his reflected image confirmed his resolve. After struggling to get into his shoes—the special right shoe they had given him was still trouble—he left the hotel and had a cup of coffee at Murdock's drug store. Fine, it was still there. Felt good to be in a familiar place, though he didn't recognize anyone inside.

He walked tall across the street to the bank, knowing what he had to do. He had thought about it all the way home.

"Well, sure I remember you, Baker," said Wendell Hardy, manager of the Blue Bonnet Bank, Cleo Springs Branch, the only bank in town. "You were one hellava halfback in high school. Right?"

"Yessir, I guess."

Rotund, middle-aged, brassy, partly bald, Hardy sat behind a large polished wooden desk in his office, two walls of which were covered with civic plaques declaring what a good citizen he was, or some such. Everyone from the Kiwanis Club to the Girl Scouts seemed to have gone on record showing their official appreciation. Being a banker sure does win you lots of friends, especially in a small town.

Lyle told the bank manager why he had come to see him and waited for a response. Hardy appeared to ignore his comments, as if he hadn't heard them. Instead he continued, "Back in '40 and '41, I do believe, you were All-State, weren't you?"

"Yessir."

"Halfback. Right?"

"Yessir."

"Hell, I remember seeing you score three touchdowns against Wichita Falls one year. Man, you were fast and tough. Got a full football scholarship to OU, right? What happened to you?"

"The War."

"Oh, right, 'a course. Too bad. A shame. But even so, Baker, what makes you think you can come in here as big as life, after all these years and expect to get a $5,000 loan with no collateral at all? That's a big fistful of money, boy. You know, we got stockholders to answer to. We can't just go around giving out loans to anybody. Nobody's even seen you around here for…well, ten years or more."

"Mr. Hardy, sir, I was thinking…." He struggled to get it out. "Since I was in the War and all, maybe you might make an exception and loan me the money anyway."

"Look here, Baker, many Texas boys come back in '45 and '46 after the War. And we helped lots of them. Hell, the parties lasted for over a year, almost every week.

But man, it's 1951! Five, six years since the War ended. Where the hell you been?"

"I sort of lost a little time in Germany." Lyle's look said he knew the questions would come now.

"Lost a little time, eh? Well now, I guess *so*." Hardy chuckled. "Boys 'a been getting their lives back together here for quite a few years now. Lots of opportunities here. New things happening. And you been lollygaggin' in Germany since the War ended?"

"That's right, sir, in a manner of speaking." *Is he playing with me, or what?*

"In the Army?"

"Yes. No, not exactly."

"Now what does that mean?"

Baker shifted in his chair. Maybe he shouldn't have come to the bank. Maybe there was another way. But he couldn't think of any and he needed the money. Besides, he was here now; he'd see it through. "I wasn't allowed to come home," he said evenly.

He thought maybe the banker would be satisfied with that.

"You mean you were stockaded?"

"No. I mean yes, I guess."

"Christ, you don't make sense. Look, I'd really like to help you, boy, but all our loan money is committed. Why don't you get a GI loan?"

"Can't. Not eligible."

"Why not?"

Baker knew he would have to say it. He wasn't ashamed exactly, but he wasn't proud of what happened to him either. *Why does the banker have to know anyway?*

"Double D. Dishonorable Discharge." There, it was out. He felt relieved

"Dishonorable Discharge? Well now, you a coward or something?"

It's none of his business, Baker thought. But he couldn't let it end there. He had come this far. With a defiant edge he said, "I beat up an officer real bad in a bar in Stuttgart after the War. He had it coming. Almost killed him. They gave me five years in prison."

"Well now, you don't say. Why'd you do that? Drunk?"

He wanted to say "yes," and be done with it and leave. That would end the discussion. But he couldn't just walk out. "Nope." He drew a slow breath, exhaled, thought for a long moment. "That's a long story, sir, and I don't imagine it has much to do with why I'm here. I'd rather not go into it." He figured it was his memory to live with, no one else's. Too painful. He didn't want to think about it anymore. But the bank manager wouldn't let it go.

"Well now, I got time," kicking back in his chair and lighting up a cigar. "And since you're the one asking for the money, maybe you'd better just tell me about it, that is, if you still want a loan."

Baker sighed, a young man burdened by experience beyond his years. His pride tugged at him. *Why is he pushing me? Why doesn't he just say 'no loan' and be done with it? I've told him enough.*

Hardy kept looking at him, waiting, as if he were really interested. Their eyes met, held, silently measuring—two men trying to see into each other... through each other. "All right," Baker said quietly, ending the impasse, sensing something was changing.

He decided to tell what happened. It wouldn't be easy. He hadn't talked about it with anyone for a few years. But he started in, not knowing where he would stop. "After the War, I married a German girl; her folks were killed in the bombings. She had nobody anymore. We lived in a small apartment off the post and planned to come to the States soon as I got discharged."

Baker looked out the window, across the morning's bright sky, remembering. He could feel the warmth of her soft round curves against his body. A familiar ache of loneliness gripped him, an empty mold of her impression. He had no desire to continue talking. Stared out the window.

Hardy sensed Baker tightening up. "I hear you, boy. Those were tough times, for sure. But what happened to you? You ought to tell me if you want me to help. He paused. "What was her name?"

Baker spoke quietly, as if not answering. "Frieda," he said, seeing her in his mind. "She had soft, long blonde hair, the biggest blue eyes I'd ever seen, and as kind as could be."

It was more than he wanted to say, but he realized he couldn't stop there. He turned to the bank manager. "One day, on land mine demolition assignment, I got my foot pretty well blasted. They sent me to a hospital in Wiesbaden for a time. While I was there, Frieda cleaned officers' private quarters off the post to make ends meet. We were saving every penny." He paused again, mulled it over. His stomach started twisting.

"What happened was, this guy, this Captain, raped my wife in his quarters and roughed her up pretty bad. She was only nineteen. She was pregnant and lost our baby."

He looked away. His eyes narrowed, his face tightened. Hardy started to interrupt, raised his hand, as if he wanted to tell him that was enough. But Baker continued, the pitch of his voice lower, almost menacing. Something had triggered inside. He wanted to tell it all now. "When I finally caught up with him—took me six months, found him in a Stuttgart bar—he laughed, said he did it. Said, 'So what? She asked for it.' "

Baker clenched his fists, reliving the moment. "He was a big guy, but he whimpered like a baby when I punched the livin' hell outta him, first in the stomach, then his face, then his head, then his face again, over and over, till he was bloody, almost unconscious. I wanted to kill him. But I didn't. I walked away."

Hardy listened as Baker relived the beating, and nodded with apparent understanding.

Baker opened his fists. "At my Court Martial he denied even knowing her. Said it must have been someone else. They believed him. He was an officer, like I said."

He got up and walked over to the bookcase, stared at it without focusing. In a calmer, softer voice he said, "Once I was inside, I couldn't get much help out to my wife. Times were rough then for German girls who married GIs. She was sick a long time. I took care of her when I got out, best I could. She got pneumonia. Never recovered. She died a few months ago. There was no reason for me to stay there anymore. So I come home." His voice trailed off.

Heaviness slumped him. His words hung in the room like sound mobiles resonating with silent echoes.

Saying nothing, Hardy appeared to search the void, listening, as if picturing the images of Baker's story. An automobile horn beeped, an abrupt intrusion. It jarred Baker.

All this is too personal. Why am I telling all this? I don't want people's pity. That's enough. I'm leaving.

Hardy had watched him carefully and spoke now with compassion. "Boy, sorry to hear it." He heaved a sigh. "Don't you have any family here?" His tone was soft and caring. His demeanor was getting through to Baker.

Baker answered with a new voice, almost dispassionate. He couldn't retract his secrets. For some reason he didn't care anymore. If felt good to get it all out. "There was my grandmother. She passed on some time ago."

Another pause. The clock ticked in the stillness. "So what do you want the money for, son?"

Baker sensed the man might be serious and not just being nosy. He relaxed, looked out the window. "Farm," he said hopefully. "My grandpa had a small spread over near Aline. Not used in a long time." He looked back at Hardy. "But the potential is there. I want to settle back here and make a new life. I've thought about it a long time." He said with a verve that seemed to passion his earnestness. "I can work hard. I know about farming. And the foot's no problem at all. I can do it."

"Hmm ... well, I'll have to think about it. You sound like you've got your head on straight, and you *have* been through a lot. But, I don't know. We'll have to review the situation and all. At least I'd like to invite you over to dinner, son, like we used to do with most of the boys when they came home."

"That's very kind of you, sir."

"Well, wait a minute now," Hardy said, sounding a little sheepish. "I, ah, now look, Baker, I'm sorry, but I may have spoken too soon. You see ..."

It was evident something bothered the banker as he seemed to chose his words gingerly. "My wife, Penelope, she's kind of, you might say, *sensitive* about the family mixing with ah, well, you know, folks of Indian blood. Even if they were soldiers. I don't agree with her at all. Neither do my daughters. But she is my wife and I do have to respect her wishes. You understand, don't you, Baker? You are Indian, aren't you? Leastwise, part?"

Baker thought about it a moment. At least the man hadn't called him a half-breed. He appreciated that. He looked at the telephone on the desk, then at the family picture in a lacquered mesquite frame, Hardy, his wife and three beautiful young women smiling by a fireplace. He sighed resolutely, faced Hardy.

"Yessir. I'm half Pawnee." His voice heated up. "And to tell you the truth, with no disrespect to your good wife, I'm proud of it. Yes, I understand, Mr. Hardy, that's the way it still is around here. But I want to tell you, I was as good an American soldier as the next guy, and better than many of them. I was a First Sergeant, got three citations, two medals. Over there what you *did* was who you are, not where you came from, or who your folks were. I'm real sorry your wife feels that way."

"You wouldn't be carrying a chip on your shoulder, now would you? Hardy spoke slowly, not accusing Baker, but as if he really wanted to know. "Maybe being in prison doesn't let somebody feel too good about people. You still angry at the guy you beat up? And the Army for putting you in prison?"

"Sure I am. I figure the Army didn't know better. But that guy sure did. I put it all behind me, though. I found out that even doing the right thing don't mean nothin' to some people if they feel threatened by what you did. I did what I had to do. I can't change that. And I'm not apologizing. I served my time and never cried about it. Just thought about coming home someday with my wife. I'm here now, without her. Guess I can take on whatever I have to."

A shot rang out, a sharp crack that seemed like it was right outside the front window. Baker dove to the carpeted floor. "Whoa, man," said Hardy with a chuckle. "It's only a truck backfiring."

Baker got up slowly, somber. Stood tall and brushed himself off, as if he had come up off the ground. Mustering his pride he said, "Mr. Hardy, sir, no need to invite me to dinner. That's no problem. I understand. I appreciate your time. I know you're a busy man and a good one, too, I expect. But if you'll excuse me, I'll be gettin' on now."

"Hold on, *Mister* Baker. Hold your horses. Tell you what." Hardy reached into his desk drawer and extracted some papers. "You fill out these forms, Mister Lyle Baker. And we'll just see what we can do about a loan, and about *dinner at my house,* too. And maybe tomorrow we could take a drive out to your grandpa's place. Could be the answer to the whole problem."

"Thank you, sir. That's most kind. Then there's one more thing maybe I ought to tell you."

"Oh? And what's that?" Hardy eyed him with a guarded look.

"I enlisted right after football season my last year here. I never waited to graduate. I intend to do that soon as I can, while I'm working the farm, and keep on taking courses afterwards. Thought I'd better tell you first. Will that interfere with me getting a loan?"

"Could pose a problem." Hardy's tone seemed serious. "You'd have your hands full running a farm and studying, probably need some help. However, maybe I do have a suggestion in that case."

Baker's faced tightened again as he braced himself to hear the hitch. "What's that, sir?"

The banker gazed at the family picture on his desk, seemed to study it, touched the frame tenderly and said, "I know a fine young gal, very well, as matter of fact. Name's Emily. She teaches school here. A fine young woman. Graduated from OU, as a matter of fact. She's single of course, and I'm thinking, she just might be willing to be your tutor."

Baker looked at the picture. He tried to speak, but no words would come out.

**

Kiss The Blarney Stone...
The Quest_____

"Taxi. Hey, taxi. *Weeo-weet.*" With a full pucker Matt Conway whistles, aiming with determination at a cab headed in the opposite direction on the far side of the plaza. The black and green taxi slows, finds a daring opening across six lanes of noon-hour traffic, executes a gutsy u-turn on Patrick Street, downtown Cork's busiest shopping destination, and pulls to the curb right in front of the Conways.

Matt and Meredith can hardly believe it. They have been trying for ten minutes to hail a cab. With a sense of victory and relief, they hustle into the back seat. Matt closes the door behind him, feeling somewhat heroic, saying to his wife, "Pretty good whistle, eh sweetie?" She doesn't respond.

He leans forward without pausing and says to the driver, "Can you take us to Blarney Castle, please? Thank you."

They settle back into the comfy leather seat and relax. The downtown commercial center of Cork, Ireland is bustling on this warm sunny day, an unseasonably balmy one for Ireland, even in July. Matt is surprised at the nice weather. After all, isn't this the land of mist and rain? Why else would the grass be so green? It's the Ole' Sod of sweaters-in-summer, chilling fog, and quaint taverns where visitors and locals alike tell each other exaggerated stories while sipping Ireland's nourishing national treasure, Guinness Stout. Or so Matt believes.

The couple's cruise ship is docked for the day at the nearby town of Cobh, the port-of-call for Cork. In the dramatic yesteryears of transatlantic crossings of ocean-going steamships, Cork was the last European stop for ships sailing to the States. It was also the port of embarkation for passengers sailing from Ireland. This could explain why, when asked at Ellis Island where they were from, so many early Irish immigrants said, "Cork". This also may have been the case with some of Meredith's forebears.

The Titanic made its final stop there on April 10, 1912, when hundreds of America-bound Irish passengers embarked. It was just four days before the starry night, 300 miles off the coast of Newfoundland, when the calm, unforgiving, frigid waters of the North Atlantic swallowed the "unsinkable", along with over 1500 passengers and crew.

The Conways know the story of the Titanic, having seen the movie. Actually, they know more about the Titanic than they do of their own Irish heritage. Meredith has researched her roots on the Internet for some time, but has gone as far as she can. She is determined to uncover missing, un-interneted information in Cork at the Census Bureau of Records.

Based on family stories handed down from generation to generation, she is intrigued by the possibility that one of her ancestors owned a castle somewhere in County Cork. She had told Matt she wants to find the place and maybe visit it.

Matt, on the other hand, has no interest in tracing his partly-Irish roots. What he wants most when they get to Cork is to visit Blarney Castle and see the Blarney Stone ... maybe even kiss it. Irish folk tradition says that people who kiss the Blarney Stone will have everlasting good luck and enjoy the gift of gab. Of course he doesn't believe any of that. But he is curious.

Not taking Matt's talk of the Blarney Stone seriously, Meredith had said before they got to Ireland, "You really want to do that, honey? It seems rather silly. We'll be right there in Cork where they have all the original records. It's a great opportunity to trace our roots."

"You can look for yours, but those kind of days bore the hell out of me. I really don't want to do that. I really want to go out to Blarney Castle. But maybe we can do both."

On the day they arrive in Cork, Matt goes to play a morning round of golf, arranged by the ship's shore excursion program. Meredith spends her morning searching records at the *County Cork Tourist Information Center*. Extensive documents are housed there and available for American visitors who wish to research their Irish heritage.

She is able to find the baptismal record of someone with her family name, Comiskey, from the parish archives of a church located in the nearby town of Cobh. After more searching through several large, hand-written record books, she uncovers what she is looking for: *Comiskey, Daniel, born 1821 in Cobh, County Cork.*

Following the name, more information is recorded in cursive script too ornate for her to decipher. She asks the young clerk to help her.

"Certainly, Ma'am. And what would you be wanting to know, then?"

"Well, I think this is my, great, great uncle, and he owned a castle somewhere nearby." She indicates a place on the opened page, holding her finger on the name until she is sure the clerk knows precisely where to look. "Does it say anything about him owning a castle?"

"Hmm. Ah, now, let's see. Oh yes, here 'tis. *Daniel Comiskey* … indeed, it says he was a Publican."

"Oh, good. Does that mean he owned a castle? Nearby, I hope?" Her eyes brighten.

"Ah, well then, I suppose some might call it that. He ran a pub."

"A pub?"

"Yes, Ma'am. A pub."

When they meet at noon at a pre-arranged spot in on Patrick Street, she and Matt have a good laugh as she tells him about the pub.

"The man had foresight," Matt says. "He must have been the most popular guy in town. After all, a man's pub is his castle."

"Oh, please…. "

"Heh, heh. By the way, I've never seen such smooth greens. What a beautiful golf course." He tells her he how well he played, something he usually says after golfing.

"That's nice, honey. What was your score? The real score, I mean. Not one of your creative estimations."

"You got me there. But if you must know, I didn't keep score today. Nope."

"Never heard of a golfer not keeping score."

"It was too nice a day."

"Hmm." She says no more.

At first it seems to Matt that, other than apparent mild curiosity and a certain measure of marital courtesy, Meredith is more interested in his golf score than the Blarney Stone. But later when she quizzes him about it in the cab, the conversation goes like this. "So, Matt honey, you're really serious about wanting to kiss the Blarney Stone?"

"Uh-huh."

"What on earth for?"

"Ah, I don't know. I think it would be fun. And we're here, aren't we?"

"Sounds unsanitary to me

"I'm sure they must have some kind of hygienic procedures."

"You think, huh? Why do you want to do it?"

"When I was a little kid back in Massachusetts my Irish grandmother used to tell the family about the Blarney Stone. On Thursday nights her nephew, (we called him Uncle) Johnny Donlon, would come over to the house for supper. The adults would stay gathered at the kitchen table sipping coffee long after we finished eating. They'd listen while Johnny regaled everybody with one story after another about the Old Sod and the Blarney Stone ... about magic faeries and leprechauns, and poor folks finding huge sums of money under rocks in the forest or under a bridge.

"It was great stuff," Matt continues. "The family had a good time. I'm sure they didn't believe any of it. But I was in awe. 'Sure and you must have kissed the Blarney Stone, Johnny Boy,' my Grandmother would say when he finished a tale. He'd say, 'No, darlin', I only heard about it from me parents.' Johnny was one of those voluble, natural-born storytellers, whose tales were laced with vagaries of Irish wit and culture. The sound of his brogue flowed like Irish music and rolled along with a twinkle.

"You could tell everyone loved his whimsy by the hearty laughs and cajoling that followed each story. I was about eight or nine at the time, and it never occurred to me that Uncle Johnny's tales were part folklore, part fable, and mostly imaginings decorated with his outrageous embellishments. I believed whatever he said, especially when he told me that a pony would be waiting for me in the backyard *next* Christmas morning. 'The Leprechauns will bring it themselves, for sure now. That is, unless they decide to keep it for themselves. You can never know with those little devils.' You take those things seriously when you're eight years old. Of course no pony ever appeared."

Meredith listens intently, then laughs as only a wife can. "You know, in some ways you're just as gullible now."

"You're so understanding, sweetheart. That's why I married you. And you're so gorgeous."

"Yeah, sure. Seems to me you must have already kissed the Blarney Stone with malarkey like that."

"Thank you, sweetheart."

His wife looks out her window at the bustling traffic. Matt watches the crowds of people on his side scurrying about on their lunch hour. He is relieved to be in the taxi and on their way to Blarney Castle. After a few moments they turn to each other. The realization strikes both at the same time: the taxi has not yet moved.

"Some whistle," Meredith says, sotto voce.

Matt speaks up, "Driver, can you please take us to Blarney Castle?"

A heavy silence follows. Even the sounds of city traffic don't seem to penetrate into the cab. Finally, there comes from the driver a long sigh. After a few labored deep breaths, which the Conways can plainly hear, he uncorks with, "Why the hell do you want to go there, then? If you were to ask me and hadn't gotten into my taxi first, I would have said you should be walking across the street, past that bank on the corner ... see it over there?

"Go down the block, turn left at the end, and you'll find a very good sandwich shop. Not expensive. Ask them to make you a couple of nice sandwiches. Wrap them up, get something to drink, and be off to the lovely Irish countryside with your wife. Sit yourselves down on a hill somewhere and have yourselves a lovely picnic. Enjoy the beautiful Irish scenery. There's nothing like it in the world. Especially on a day like today."

He becomes a bit strident. "That's what you should be doin', now, not traipsin' off to see some stupid piece of rock with thousands of tourists and buses and all that commotion and hubbub there. I can't for the life of me understand why all you folks run to Blarney Castle when you come here. Why do all these ships and tour companies send people there? It's a sin. Really it is."

The Conways are floored. The driver sounds like a poet, or maybe he's a spokesperson for Greenpeace. But driving a cab? Obviously he means every word.

After a thoughtful pause Matt offers, "It's all about business, I guess. Tour operators can't make any money if they tell the ship's tourists to go on a picnic. Neither can you."

"Well now then, even so, that's no way to be experiencing Ireland. It truly is a beautiful land. You should be finding that out while you're visiting."

The taxi still hasn't moved. "You're right," says Matt with extra politeness, "but our ship is here for only a few hours, and we got a late start. Many Americans have heard about the Blarney Stone since they were kids. So with only a few hours to spend, we thought we'd like to go there and see it. Could you take us? Please?"

After a long pause, in which it appears to Matt and Meredith that the driver is actually considering options, he says, "Well, all right, then. But don't be surprised if you're disappointed." He shrugs with resignation, and they're finally on their way. Matt and his wife look at each other, trying desperately to stifle giggles, amazed by the driver's candor. Something is definitely different about him.

Matt loses himself in thoughts of his past. Sooner or later the kitchen stories always got around to the Blarney Stone. His grandmother would eventually sum up the evening saying that their lives would have been different if only they had kissed the Blarney Stone before they left Ireland. Little Matthew decided back then it had to be some kind of magic stone.

As a kid he could just imagine this huge, dark castle somewhere in Ireland, with a secret dungeon. And in the dungeon, in the middle of its stone floor would be a round opening. You could look down deep to the bottom of the pit. There, a sharply pointed stone sat like a fierce stalagmite pointing up at you. You had to be lowered down head first and be held by your ankles in order to kiss it, if you were brave enough. And if you did, you'd get this great reward forever. It would be like wining the Irish Sweepstakes.

He resolved that someday when he grew up, if ever he got to Ireland, he'd find the Blarney Stone. He could just imagine himself being lowered head first, feet tied with a rope—attached to a winch, or maybe held by some local giant who would dangle him down—until he could touch the Stone with his lips. He wondered if the winch ever failed or if the giant ever let anyone go. He figured that would mean death by brain impalement.

"I know it's all baloney," he finally says to his wife, "but I've always wanted to see the Blarney Stone and maybe even kiss it. Is that so unreasonable?"

"Oh honey, go kiss the rock already," his wife says. "I think it's silly, but do it if you want to."

It is a beautiful, thirty-minute drive out to the village of Blarney. The four-lane highway takes them past lush green rolling fields and hills, replete (they kid each other) with Irish cows, Irish sheep, and Irish grass, of course. They marvel and point and in general are sincerely impressed. The soft, bright shade of green is a color they have not experienced before.

Matt mentions to the driver about Meredith having kin roots in County Cork, "probably in nearby Cobh," and that they had had to give up the search because of their limited time today.

"Oh, they were from Cobh then, were they," the cab driver says. "Well, have you tried the phone book, then? What's the surname? There must be someone here that knows of them. People don't move around that much here these days, ya know."

"Comiskey," the couple chimes in together, and no, they haven't tried the phone book.

"Ah, Comiskey is it then? There's not many Comiskeys anymore. So someone should be knowing them around Cobh." Before they know it, he pulls off the highway and drives up to a gas station convenience store just off the highway. "I'll be right back," he says as he gets out and goes in. He returns a few moments later with a phone book, gets into the cab and searches the pages for Comiskey.

"Let's see now, in Cobh … Comiskey. Ah, here 'tis … Comiskey." There are fifteen Comiskeys. He takes out his cell phone and starts dialing, saying to the Conways something like he hopes they didn't mind his trying to help.

"No, no," they say, astounded. "It's very kind of you. But you really shouldn't. We hate to impose."

"Oh, no problem a'tall. After all, to come all this way, and not be finding them…." He dials again and listens to the ringing. After he has tried three numbers with no response, the Conways insist that it is more than kind of him, but that they cannot ask him for anything further, and perhaps they should be on their way to the Castle before it closes.

"Alright then, yes of course," he says. Then turning and looking at Meredith, he says, "Now remember, you never saw me do this." With that, he rips out the page (page 132) with *Comiskeys* from the phone book and hands it to her, then returns the book to the convenience store. Again, they are amazed with the man.

They can hardly believe it. "What's your name?" Matt asks when he returns.

"Oh, yes, of course, my name. It's Shamus. Shamus O'Shamus. You can call me Shamus, or O'Shamus, for that matter. I'm the same person. I always have been, as far as I know. Sorry I couldn't be of more help. I do hope you have good luck finding your kin."

At the little village of Blarney, the cab pulls into one of the many parking lots jammed with tour buses. "First I'll show you where the entrance to the Castle grounds is," says Shamus. "It's a bit confusing, so be paying attention, now. See where I'm pointing? Just past that big tree, then off to the right and over the hill. The gate is there. There'll be a long line.

"Now I should tell you, taxis don't usually come out here unless they're called. So give a thirty-minute warnin' when you're done lookin' and someone will be here to pick you up. Just go into Christy's Tavern there, have a nice Irish beer—there's nothing like it—and use the free phone at the bar."

He gives them his card with the number of the Taxi Company on it." And one more thing, watch out for the fancy Blarney Gift Store over there. It's a rip-off for sure. It's for tourists who don't know any better. Very nice quality, but you can buy the same things in town for half the price."

The fare comes to a little under twenty Euros. Matt hands him thirty, and tells him to please keep the change.

"Oh no, that's entirely too much, now," says the driver. "That's not right. I'll be taking three (Euros) for a proper tip, if that's okay with you." He returns a five-Euro bill to Matt.

"You sure?" Matt says, almost flabbergasted. Never in his life has he heard a taxi driver say the tip is too much. He stares at the driver, waiting for a response.

"Absolutely. I can't be doing that, now," says Mr. Shamus Whatever.

"How come?"

"I have a habit. At night when I go home, I need to be able to say to myself: I didn't try to fool anybody today or do anything to hurt anyone. I only tried to help them."

"Well you've sure helped us. We'll never forget your kindness. Did you ever kiss the Blarney Stone?"

"Of course not. Not me, and I've lived here all my life. That's for tourists. It's a bunch of baloney. Have a beautiful day now. And God bless you both."

"Thank you, Mr. O'Shamus," says Meredith.

"Shamus to you, me luv."

"Thank you, Shamus."

Giving her a wink and a nod and a casual wave, he drives off.

"My God," says Matt, "what a most remarkable man. It feels like we've just met the real Santa Claus."

They wait in line, pay the admission, and enter the castle's beautiful hilly grounds. After a bit of a hike up a short, steep hill, along a winding path, they climb around the 700-year-old remains of the structure and take the obligatory pictures of each other, thus proving to whomever (and maybe to themselves later) that 'we were here'.

There is a long line, a one-hour wait, queued up to enter the tower parapet, the inside of which is beyond the entrance and hidden from view. Matt is ready to brave the challenge with heroic posture. He resolves to submit himself to the awaiting challenges he has imagined, whatever they are.

But no! Pictures at the entrance reveal there isn't a darkened dungeon inside after all. Nor is there a mystical pointed sword-of-stone poised to split your skull in half if you slipped. Instead, photographs outside the entrance show tourists kissing the stone, no doubt to encourage business for the photo concessionaire. One photo shows a woman leaning over backwards with a large man supporting her gently—his hand under the small of her back—as she pokes her head though a large opening into the turret wall. The next picture shows her stretching her neck up a bit and kissing a flat round stone in the turret ceiling.

What? What a sham, thinks Matt. Where is the challenge? Where is the danger? Where is the rope and winch or the giant? This isn't *his* Blarney Stone, the stuff of fables, the medieval torture challenge he knows should be there. It is nothing more than a small stone plastered into the low ceiling of a hole in old wall, a mediocre tourist attraction. Nothing like what he has envisioned from his uncle Johnny's description years ago.

The scoundrel, Matt now thinks. He feels deceived and disappointed, crushed, actually. If there is a redeeming aspect to this disappointment, however, it is that Matt has unmasked a myth firmed in his mind from his youth, though he has not set out to do that. He has unfrocked a fraud. Laid bare a lie. Stomped on a serpent of deceit. The truth finally is out of the bottle. But Matt resents the fact that something has been taken from him, something personal, something mysterious, something he looked forward to, to savor, to dream about. He doesn't like it at all that reality has snuffed out his dream. Gone is the awe and magic of 'what if.'

Matt Conway loses all desire to kiss the Blarney Stone. His lingering infatuation with the idea is suddenly *interruptus completum.* He will forego the slurping of the fabled slab and its promised reward. Kissing the stone doesn't seem necessary or even desirable to him anymore.

"Aw forget it," he says to Meredith, "I've changed my mind."

"What? You're kidding, me, right? We've come all this way and now you're not going to smooch the stupid rock? After what you've told me? And we're next in line! Well, I will then."

"Oh, come, honey," he says, "it's just that it doesn't seem important to me anymore. I don't know … I guess it isn't what I expected. Maybe someone did me a favor."

But even as he says this, she extracts her lipstick from her purse, twists it open with one hand, the dexterous move of an expert, and quickly applies an extra thick layer of *Flame*. She turns to him, puckers an exaggerated kiss, then saunters into the entrance. There a tall, rather handsome, dark-haired young man waits to escort and assist each tourist, one at a time.

After several minutes Meredith emerges smiling, brushing back her long auburn hair.

"So how was kissing the Blarney Stone, Sweetheart?" Matt says. "Or should I say, *the sham-rock? Heh, heh.*" He thinks for sure he has her then.

She looks at him wide-eyed and innocent, as only a woman can do. "Why, Sweetie, what Blarney Stone?" she says, as she reapplies her lipstick then strolls a few steps to a nearby ice cream vender.

Matt stands watching her. She always amazes him. It is as if she has really said to him, "Too bad for you, Buster, you blew it this time." And he knows she'd be right.

Later when he calls from Christy's to order a cab he introduces himself to the operator and tells him how impressed he is with the thoughtful service he and his wife received earlier from one of their drivers.

"Thank you, then, Mr. Conway. I'm so glad you appreciated the service. And what would be the driver's name again, please?"

"Shamus O'Shamus," Matt says. "He gave us a card. Said to call you."

"Sir, we thank you for calling. Very kind of you, of course. We'll send a taxi right out for you. It will take thirty minutes."

"Thank you."

"But I'm afraid, sir, there is no driver here by that name. Never has been."

**

A Letter...
In the Amazon Rainforest___

1914 April, probably. I am not certain.

The River of Doubt
Somewhere in the Amazon Rain Forest
Brazil, SA

Timothy Wilton
Brown University
Providence, Rhode Island
United States of America

My Dear Son,

I recount these events to you that you may know what happened to me, should you by some miracle ever receive this letter. Parts of this record will no doubt be unpleasant for you to read. Having said that, you must forgive me if I begin with an incident that I consider essential to the story.

I remember the day my toes turned black. First the nails, then the skin, the tips, the sensitive sides, the unprotected tops, even the callous pads underneath, until in just a few days my toes looked like half-charred, half-eaten knots of bone and flesh. It was just the beginning.

The treacherous microbes that invaded my body must have taken a particular liking to me. It wasn't long before my feet and ankles were corrupted by a strange black scourge. Whatever it was ate my flesh, and was making its way toward my knees. There seemed to be no stopping it. Oddly enough, there was no pain. I am at a loss to explain why. Soon I became disoriented with fever.

On the day I was afflicted, I had been in the forest categorizing the fascinating varieties of unknown species of flora. I must say this was a botanist's dream. It should be noted: the realization that I was the first civilized man in all the world to encounter the incredible plant life of this remote area of the rain forest brought me to a high state of euphoria.

I was but a short distance from our camp when Indian natives attacked our site. I heard the screams of our men—there were only three left. I ran away, headlong, twisting and turning into the jungle until I was at a safe distance. For a time I could hear whooping and shouting. Then all was still. I hid for a time, listening, stricken with fear, not noticing that I was standing in a mucky swamp. It was here, I believe, that my pores were invaded by some mysterious microbe.

Friendly Indians found me days later wandering about, delirious. After much verbal commotion, which I could not understand, they laid me down on large leaves, the likes of which I had not encountered before in the jungle. They stripped me of my clothing. Several of them then began urinating profusely on my legs and feet. The pain was incredible. I screamed in agony and disbelief. They continued. The smell of urine and the swarm of flies my putridity attracted made me want to vomit. I must have passed out.

I must rest now. I will continue later.

The next day—
You know, of course, I was selected to join the Roosevelt-Rondon Scientific Expedition to the Amazon rain forest because I am a botanist of some note. The Smithsonian Institute contracted me to categorize the territory's flora and take photographs to support my notes. I don't think, however, I ever

shared my private thoughts with you about going on this expedition.

The President initiated the project in cooperation with New York's American Museum of Natural History and the Museo Social in Buenos Aires. True, the expedition's purpose was to further the development of mankind by charting vast areas of the Brazilian rain forest. Its primary mission was to attempt passage of the unexplored River of Doubt from its head waters in the high plateaus to its eventual entrance into the mighty Amazon River tributary system, probably more than 1,000 miles distant. No one knew for sure.

But to my way of thinking, and bearing in mind Mr. Roosevelt's gregarious spirit, I believe he had in purpose the thought that the adventure would be an interesting and useful diversion after the devastating experience of his failed 1912 re-election bid for the Presidency. (I do believe the new President, Mr. Woodrow Wilson, will prove to be a preferable choice to Mr. Taft. I am optimistic about him.)

T. Roosevelt took the loss very dearly. Even so, we always referred to him as Mr. President. You must know he had a high sense of self and adventure. But I am sure he experienced far more adventure on this expedition than he ever anticipated.

The River of Doubt, so christened Rio Da Duvida by Rondon, is well beyond the navigable reaches of the Amazon system itself. There is no known boat passage. As we discovered, the dark river often narrows, bordered by jungles and jagged cliffs and is fraught with perilous rapids. There are no settlements.

Up to this point, the only inhabitants we had seen in this vast wilderness were a few reclusive, primitive natives, whose culture seems more like that of the Stone Age.

But I digress. We set out jolly enough, sailing from New York October 4, 1913 in a celebratory mood on the steamship Vandyck, with stops in Barbados, Bahia, and Rio de Janeiro. We rounded the southern tip of South America and proceeded up the west coast to Santiago, Chile. There we transferred to a shallow-river steamer and crossed into Brazil, navigating the wide Paraguay River upstream. After several days we disembarked at a small telegraph frontier town (Tapirapoa, I think it was called) and began making the difficult 400-mile overland trek through the descending Andean plateaus of southwestern Brazil.

It was an arduous journey. But the expectations of exploring an uncharted river energized us.

When we reached the terminus of our land journey, the headwaters of the River of Doubt, it was necessary for some of the expedition party to return to civilization as planned. There were simply too many to make the canoe passage. We bid farewell to many guides and porters. Together with the horses and carts which had carried our canoes and supplies, they began to retrace the overland route with lightened loads. I tire.

Dawn the following day—
There were enough dugout canoes for twenty of us to make the passage. We launched our five canoes, including provisions, onto the narrow headwaters and began searching our way down the uncharted river. The canoes sat very low in the water with about four inches of freeboard.

We soon learned that highlands meant fast water and rapids. There were many days of portages, often twice a day, even three, sometimes after only a few hundred yards of the river. We had to carry the heavy, water-logged canoes around unexpected falls and violent rapidos, hacking through tangled brush, even felling trees to clear a way for the canoes. This required negotiating the loads up steep forested terrain. It was an exhausting effort.

Eventually, we entered the dark interior of the Brazilian rain forest where we encountered even more formidable obstacles and unanticipated dangers, most of them biological.

We followed the narrow, twisting river for over two months, though we had not progressed as far as we had hoped. By that time none of us was in the best of shape. Fatigued, plagued by vermin, bugs, *poisonous plants, snakes and ever-present mosquitoes, each day became more difficult for us. Every night we camped close to the riverbank and tried to protect ourselves from the environment. Rains came in torrents, saturating clothing that clung to our skin. We could not seem to ever get dry. The men were ill with fever.*

I must say the President's fine demeanor was at all times exemplary. He remained spirited, that is until he became seriously ill. Alas, racked with malaria fever and a serious infection from a leg gash he suffered on the rapids, and in grave danger of death, he agreed to the decision to evacuate him. The next day, accompanied by his son Kermit, Colonel Rongon, George Cherrie (the naturalist) and two Brazilian guides, he departed—all of them in the one remaining canoe. We could only hope they would be able to negotiate the many hundreds of miles left on the dark water and reach a connecting Amazon tributary. We knew they must accomplish this in time to save the President's life. We said goodbyes with fervent hopes for the President's recovery.

I remained behind with three others. The rest of our Brazilian porters, exhausted 'cameradas', had abandoned the expedition a few days earlier, after four canoes, two of which carried our already diminished quantity of food and supplies, were lost in the treacherous 'rapidos'. We were to undertake the building of another canoe and follow the evacuation team as soon it was completed.

One can only hope the President's party finds its way to civilization, although the chances of this, I feel, are slim. On the other hand, with Colonel Rondon being such an intrepid military explorer, one who has had extensive jungle experience, perhaps they will make it.

I must rest now.

About two weeks later—

Timothy, forgive my prolonged interruptions. I can remember only some of these happenings, since much of the time lately I have been struck with recurring malaria fever, thanks to those infernal giant mosquitoes. They can suck three times their body weight in blood, infecting you as they gorge. They are so fat and slow by the time they finish feasting, it is easy to swat them. By then it is too late.

Getting back to the day of attack by the Indians. My cameras and notes, except for a notebook and papers I carried with me in my small knapsack, (it is on that paper that I write this letter) were destroyed in the attack. Fortunately, I had given several roles of film to Colonel Rondon just before he left with T.R. and the others. Perhaps someday the photographs will find the light of curious eyes upon them.

As for the Indians who found me in the jungle, they brought me back to their little village, though I *have no recollection of this. Days later, I could not tell how many, (it turned out to be several weeks) I awoke in the steaming tropic heat, lying nude in a hut, thirsty, perspiring, exhausted, wondering where I was.*

A tall, unclothed Indian woman, who wore her black hair long and parted down the middle, gave me water and some fruit. Her body was decorated with necklaces of black vegetable beads strung around her neck, wrists, waist and ankles. She carefully smeared some kind of plant extract onto my legs and the rest of my body, rubbing lightly in slow, circular motions. It was cool and soothing. I fell back to sleep. I remained uncovered. Every day for many weeks she continued the treatment, feeding me, washing me with wet leaves and applying the extract.

One day she helped me to my feet. I nearly fell, but she continued to steady me until I was able to stand a bit. Others in the small group gathered around. I was wobbly but my legs, though very thin, seemed to be healing. The black flesh was gone. New pink skin was forming. Though weak, I felt no pain. The miraculous healing extract also protected me from insects, which were dying to have a feast, I am sure.

I was in a small Indian camp of about ten rectangular huts, each covered with what looked like banana leaves. The enclave was most likely part of the Cinta Larga tribe, deep-forest Brazilian natives who had been friendly to our expedition several miles upstream, far from the place where we last made camp. We often sensed the presence of Indians watching us from the forest but were never able see them.

The Cinta Larga could also be fierce protectors of their territory against intruders. We had been warned to watch out for them by guides.

After many weeks, the Cinta Larga brought me back to our campsite, about fifty feet from the bank of the river. They helped look for anything that could be of value to me. Nothing was to be found. The attacking tribe, probably the Nhambiquara (although I cannot be sure—it just could just as well have been the very Indians who rescued me) had pillaged everything. There was no sign of my three companions. Most likely they had been killed in the attack, carried off, and fed to the piranha, a favorite punishment for captured members of warring tribes. Forgive me. I must rest again.

Five days later, or so—

It must be months since I said goodbye to the President's party. Yet for some time, even though alone, except for the Indians, I have remained optimistic about the possibilities of recovering and making a dugout attempt on the river. I have not let myself become dispirited. For that is the least desirable solution for any problem.

However, although my legs have healed sufficiently, the malaria fever has now returned, this time more violently than ever. Before our supplies were lost we barely had enough quinine to keep fevers under control And now there are no longer medications at all to help, even though the Indian cures seem to benefit them. Perhaps the Cinta Larga have developed immunity to malaria.

I am now long past the point at which any attempt to build a canoe can be made. I am not one to give up easily. But I am afraid I delayed too long in this undertaking, waiting for my legs to become stronger. Each day the fever gets worse and I become weaker. I can no longer sit up and breathing has become difficult. I have only brief moments of lucidity. I know it is just a question of time.

At least the black rot that struck me (together with its putrid smell) is gone. This in itself is a blessing for which I am grateful.
I rest....

The moon was most impressive last night. I awoke in a haze from my fever to see its glow, thinking of it doing the same over Washington.

My son, it is obvious there is no chance for me. Yet I do not despair, for ...

Sometime later—

If the President and Rondon manage to reach the Amazon (I pray they have) maybe someday there *will be another expedition. I will try to leave this letter with the Cinta Larga. Perhaps it will find its way to you. I can but hope.*

I awake—

I want to tell you so much more, but my ebbing strength permits little further discourse. I say good, goodbye now. Please know this has been the experience of my life. I ...   it has been an honor to share this adventure with such brave men and to discover so many unknown w o n d e r s of the world, both ***beau ti ful and sin is ter. You must know that I have no regrets, except the re a l i z a t i on that I will never see you again. My wish is that you have a full life, and that you find j o y in doing w h a t ever it is y o u*** *must do, as I have done.*

My lo ve to you   a N d m y b l e s s i n g s always.
y o u r fAthe r,
E v e r e t t   C. W i l t o n

This letter was recovered in 1992, rolled and sealed in a bamboo tube, in a *Cinta Larga* village somewhere in the Amazon interior along the *Rio Roosevelt*.

**

Author's Note

A Letter in the Amazon Rainforest is a work of fiction based on events of the 1913-14 Roosevelt-Rondon Scientific Expedition to the Amazon basin.

Seven months after departing the United States, a weak and ailing Theodore Roosevelt returned, sailing into New York harbor aboard the steamship Adrian to a hero's welcome. His devoted son Kermit had brought him home.

In 1920 a second expedition was wiped out by Indians, the *Cinta Larga*, it is thought.

In 1992 Theodore Roosevelt's great-grandson, Tweed Roosevelt, with the help of twenty men and women, mounted a well-planned expedition to the Amazon basin. He successfully retraced the entire route his great-grandfather's expedition had taken eighty years before to explore the 1,000 mile-long River of Doubt, which had been re-named *Rio Roosevelt*.

***

GENE HULL

SLICE OF LIFE, Our Ways and Days, is Gene Hull's third book.

His first, *GOING TO COURT,* a four-color illustrated collection of Tennis Poetry, was selected for the International Tennis Hall of Fame in Newport, Rhode Island.

His second book, *HOOKED ON A HORN, Memoirs of Recovered Musician,* earned the *2006 Literary Prize for Memoir* awarded by the Florida Writers Association.

A former professional musician, Gene was an alto saxophonist and multi-reed player with Duke Ellington and other bands in the Post Swing era. He was a touring bandleader and a Las Vegas Music Director for several international celebrities. Following his music career, his innovations as Senior Entertainment Producer for Royal Caribbean Cruise Lines production shows and ice shows help set a new high standard for cruise ship entertainment.

Gene is a graduate of the University of Notre Dame with additional studies at Juilliard, Fairfield University and the Creative Writing Program of Florida International University. He resides on Florida's Treasure Coast where he is President of the Treasure Coast Writers Guild.

His website is www.genehull.com

He can be contacted via email: genehull@msn.com

Printed in the United States
120644LV00004B/103-150/P